HAUNTING HOODRAT

IRON VEX MC: NEW YORK CITY #8

ELIZABETH KNOX

IRON VEX
NEW YORK

Haunting Hoodrat

This book is a work of fiction. The names, characters, places, and incidents are all products of the author's imagination and are not to be construed as real. Any resemblances to persons, organizations, events, or locales are entirely coincidental.

Haunting Hoodrat. Copyright © 2022 by Elizabeth Knox. All rights reserved. No part of this book may be used or reproduced in any manner whatsoever without written permission from the author, except in the case of brief quotations used in articles or reviews. For information, contact E. Knox.

Editing: Kim Lubbers, Knox Publishing

Proofreading: Marybeth Higgins, Knox Publishing

Formatting: E.C. Land, Knox Publishing

Cover Designer: Charli Childs, Cosmic Letterz Cover Design

Photographer: Dante Dellamore, Dante Dellamore Photography

Models: Robert & Katie

❀ Created with Vellum

PROLOGUE

Hoodrat

An intense pressure builds up in my chest. This is where Giada and I were supposed to meet. I don't understand what she could be doing that she's not here. I clench my fists over and over, trying to release some of this tension.

I check my watch again to make sure that I'm not too early or too late. The last time I spoke with her, she was excited to come see me today. But maybe I had it wrong. Maybe she's too upset that I've been spending so much time at the club. I've already told her that since I'm prospecting, I don't have much time, and she seemed to be okay with it. If she's not showing up now, I have. I think maybe she's pissed

I've always put my duties at the clubhouse before her. No woman likes coming in second.

"Papi, are you hungry. Do you want me to make you an enchilada?" Maria, the cook of the best Mexican food truck in the borough, tilts her head to the side, confused as to why I haven't ordered yet. I'm usually on my third taco by now.

"No, I'm good, thanks." I give her the best smile that I can offer right now. It's not much. Giada has never done anything like this before. I'm starting to get fucking nervous.

I pull out my phone again and check my messages. There's nothing from her. I have already texted her three times and called about six times. This time when I try to call her, the line gives me that generic message about the phone no longer being in service.

"What the fuck! That shit can't be right. I just fucking spoke to her yesterday. That can't be right."

I try to call her number again, and I get the same message. That pressure in my chest rises up into my head, consuming my every thought. Something is wrong.

I quickly jump onto my bike and beeline straight for her house.

I park my bike behind a parked car to stay

hidden. I don't usually come over here because I know how shit can get with her parents. Today though, I really don't give a fuck. Somebody's going to tell me what the hell is going on.

Knocking on the door with as much restraint as I can muster, I wait for a few minutes for Giada to come to the door. After the first round of knocking, when nobody answered, I beat on the door harder. There are fucking lights on inside, and I see the cars in the garage, so I know someone's home.

If they think I'm going to give up and just leave, they are out of their minds.

"I know someone's fucking in there. Come to the door or I'm going to break it down," I yell out before I take a step back, ready to do exactly as I say. Just as I brace myself for the impact, the door swings open.

"What are you doing on my front step." Giada's father steps into my space and forces me to move back.

"Sir, I'm not trying to be disrespectful, but I'm worried about Giada. I've been calling her all morning, and she hasn't answered any of my calls. She hasn't returned any of my texts either." I stand with my hands behind my back the same way I would if I was standing in front of my president or another authority figure. The last thing I need right now is for her parents to think I'm a threat.

Giada's father sighs, "There's nothing wrong with her. She's not your concern anymore." He tries to turn and go back into the house, but I grab hold of his arm to stop him.

What the fuck? What is that supposed to mean?

"I don't understand. What do you mean she's not my concern anymore?" I let go of him quickly but take a step forward. Giada means too much to me to just let whatever is happening go.

"What is there not to understand." Her father squints his eyes at me, and I can see the color rising on his face. His entire stance says that he's ready to fight. If I swing now, Giada will never forgive me.

"Sir, can I just talk to Giada, and I'll be on my way," I speak through clenched teeth.

A slight snarl rises on his face, "No, there's no way that you can speak with her. She's not here."

That pressure inside of me threatens to explode, and I feel the sweat pouring down my face.

"What do you mean she's not here? Where did she go?"

"Giada doesn't wanna see you anymore. She's moved on to bigger things. We dropped her off at college last night. I'm sure she would appreciate it if you would just leave her alone. Now." He takes his hand and places it in the middle of my chest. I looked down at his arm and envisioned all the many ways that I could break it in two. I hold my composure by the very last threads, "You can get off my property before I call the cops. I'm sure someone with your background wouldn't want the authorities to get involved, am I right?"

I open my mouth to speak, but I know whatever I say is going to fall on deaf ears. Her parents never wanted us to be together. They never wanted to find out anything about me. I take a step back, shaking my head before I turn on my heel and get back to my bike.

Disbelief and sadness wash through me.

She's really gone. How could she do that to me? How could she leave and not even fucking tell me?

I wanna go off the rails. I want to go back to her house and knock on every one of her windows until I have some answers. The problem is if I were her, I would have done the same. Her parents are right to say she's going on to better things. I always knew it was a possibility that she would get tired of all my bullshit and go. I just never assumed it would be now.

I started my bike and peeled out from in front of

her house, leaving the memory of what we had and what we could've had behind me. Now that she's gone, my only priority is the club. It's time to move on with my life the same way she did.

With nothing and no one holding me back.

CHAPTER ONE

GIADA

Eleven years later . . .

I open my eyes with a start. Sucking in a huge lung full of air. I look up to the ceiling trying to get a hold of my surroundings. When my vision clears, I let out a strangled sob, and deep inside of me, another part of my soul dies.

Every morning when I wake up, I always think it's just a bad dream. Some fucked up nightmare that I'll wake up from. I'll wake up and see Hoodrat laying right next to me. It's never a dream. This fucked up prison is my life.

I sit up in the bed, turning around to see where my first meal is set. No matter what time I wake up, there's always a platter with something waiting for me. When I first got here, I thought maybe they were doing something to the food. It didn't make sense that they would go through all the effort of making three-course breakfasts and extravagant lunches just for a prisoner. After a while, though, I give in and just eat what they give me.

I find the tray on my left side, with a thermos of weak coffee. Just how I like it.

As far as prisons go, I must admit this one is really breathtaking. The house is situated on a large piece of land someplace I believe, in upstate New York. I've never actually been able to check since I can't leave.

Eleven years.

At least, I think it's been 11 years. The days seem to merge into one another now. All I know is I've lived here basically alone except for the staff and some security. The doors and windows are all locked. There's no phone, there's no computer. There's nothing here that would allow me to contact the outside world. So every day, I wake up in my own pretty prison, waiting for the chance to get out. Waiting for the day, Hoodrat comes to save me. I'm never going to give up on him, the same way he'll never give up on me.

After I have a small amount of breakfast, I do a few yoga poses simply to stretch out my underused muscles. Then I walk over to the large floor-to-ceiling window just to see what the day looks like.

My breath gets caught in my throat when I see a car I've never seen before in the circular driveway.

People never visit. Anything that has to be done is done by the help that works here. A feeling of intense excitement starts to bubble inside of my body.

What if somebody called about the house. What if those are cops trying to do a wellness check on somebody in here. It could be Hoodrat here to find me.

All of the most extreme thoughts on who the car could belong to pass through my mind. Logically, I know most of them are unlikely, but the thought of being able to get out of here makes me hope.

I quickly drag on a pair of lounge pants and a T-shirt before I walk out of my room and into the long ornate hallway. The plush carpet cushions my feet, so there's no sound when I'm walking. There are cameras all around. I know if anyone goes looking, they'll see me walking here. I just can't let this opportunity go by. If someone is here that might be able to help me, I need to get their attention.

My hands shake as I hear the deep tenor of a man's voice. I don't know who it belongs to, but I know it's not anyone that lives here.

I pick up the pace, wanting to make sure I get a set of eyes on whoever that person is. It will only take seconds for me to alert them that I need help.

I turn down the next hallway, following the sound of the man's voice and completely ignore my surroundings. I don't have time to play cautiously. As I get closer to the main part of that area, a small twinge of fear tickles the base of my spine. Whoever that voice belongs to doesn't live here, but I know I've heard it before.

It's not Hoodrat, and it's not my father. So who could it be?

I take a chance and slowly stick my head around the corner just to see who's there. Turns out I should've stayed in bed.

"Ah, Giada, how nice of you to join us. I was beginning to think you were going to sleep the whole day away." A man I've only seen once before gets up out of his chair and comes strolling in my direction. With every one of his steps, goosebumps pop up on my arms. The first time I met him, I had the same reaction. He gives me the absolute fucking creeps.

"What does it matter if I sleep the day away? It's not like I do anything anyway." I cross my arms over my chest and take a step back just to get away from being so close to him. It's always bothered me that I essentially have no wait to defend myself here. And if any one of the help or anyone that comes to the house decides they want to harm me, no one would actually know.

"Yes, that's true. I know it must be incredibly boring and quite unfulfilling for you to be here all this time."

"It is. I'm living out a life sentence for something I have no idea about. Honestly, I have no idea why these people won't just kill me. I'm of no use to anyone." I squeeze my biceps and feel my sharp nails trying to carve through the skin. I welcome the pain. At least I can feel that.

"Don't talk such nonsense," the man bites out. "Clearly, you're annoyed that I would even suggest somebody hurting you. You should be thankful that you're here and not someplace else. Those I have put here with you have gone to great lengths to make sure you have everything that you need. You will never want for anything."

The anger in my body rises to a peek as I take another step in his direction, my voice raising loudly as I stare into his face, "Never want for anything! Are you fucking out of your mind! I have nothing in here. Nothing. I don't know what's going on back in my old life. I haven't talked to anyone besides the people here in years. Everything I do is monitored, from when I go to take a shower to what I need to how long I sleep to when I go outside for a break. I'm a fucking caged animal in a really big cage. I don't know who you are or what you want, but I know you don't know what the fuck you're talking about."

When I finish my little spiel, my entire body is trembling with anger. And it feels good.

The man takes a second before he says anything. "Giada, you know who I am. We've met before."

"Yeah, I've seen you before. Of course, that doesn't mean I remember who the fuck you are." I roll my eyes and only catch the very edges of his distasteful face.

"I see you still haven't learned how unattractive that filthy mouth of yours is."

I nearly fall over laughing, "You've got to be shitting me. Do you think I'm going to sit here and play the proper lady when I'm being held here against my will? On what planet do you live?"

He huffs out a breath and shakes his head, "I had hoped things would be a little different the next time I came here, but I see that not much has changed. My name is Luigi."

"Well, Luigi, since you've been here before, I'm sure you're here again this time for something. If you could just tell me what that something is, I can be on with my day. My very exciting day of walking around the same house looking at the same walls, eating the same food, and going back to sleep in the same bed." I give him a tight smile and wait for him to say whatever it is that he has to say, so he can get out.

"I think maybe you'd want to be a little nicer to me." A smug smirk crosses his face, and he narrows his eyes at me.

"Why is that?"

"Like you said, you've been here alone pretty much for all this time. If I am the only link you have to the outside world, I would think it would be in your best interest to be friendly." He lifts his hand to his chin and scratches it slowly as if he were thinking or analyzing something on my body.

My insides shutter as I think about what he means by the words friendly. Did he really come here just so he could rape me? I look around the room one last time to see if I can find something to protect myself with, but I know no matter what I do, he's going to be able to stop me before I get there. So, I continue to play along just to see what he will do.

"It may be in my best interest to be friendly, but I've never been given much reason to believe anyone will do anything to help me in here." I hold his gaze just so I can see if he makes a move.

"I can understand your hesitation, but I'm actually here to make you a deal." He lifts his head slightly and waits for my reply.

A deal? What the hell could I have that he wants to make a deal for? No, something is wrong with this whole scenario. I don't have anything for him. No information, no overwhelming wealth, no lofty connections. Still, if he wants to make a deal, I'll at least hear him out.

"What kind of deal?"

"Oh, you know, just a few different things. I'll be honest, most of them it's just me trying to get to know you." His face goes soft, and I see something that looks like affection in his eyes.

"You . . . you want to get to know me?" I can't

even hide the suspicion in my tone. No one has ever come here just wanting to get to know me.

"Yeah, I mean," he puts his hand up to the back of his neck and massages it as if he is uncomfortable, "I know you've been here a long time. I've been put in charge of a few things surrounding your stay here. Meaning I have basically had to keep tabs on you without you even knowing. I am very impressed that you would have the strength to last this long. If this were happening to someone else, they would have gone insane or tried to hurt themselves. But not you. You're so different, and I'm having a hard time staying to myself. I'm not doing anything sinister, but I would like to get to know you, and in return for you being willing to spend some time with me, I can see what I can do to make your time here more pleasant." His eyes are searching mine.

"If you think I'm so strong and you're not doing anything sinister, why don't you just let me out of here." My throat is thick with emotion.

"I can't. I'm not the only one watching."

I let my head fall forward, my chin pointing toward my chest. This seems hopeless. He thinks I'm strong, but deep down, I know it won't be long until I lose my resolve. It's been too long, and I'm just so tired.

Maybe it would be nice to have someone take an interest in me. At least somebody to talk to." What exactly did you want me to do?"

When I see the large smile appear on his face, I feel like I might've just signed a deal with the devil.

CHAPTER TWO

HOODRAT

"Everyone, I have one last order of business to talk about." Boss looks around the room and waits for everyone to give her back their undivided attention. Of course, it doesn't take long because we all know when it is time for church, it's not time to play around.

"I've been talking back-and-forth with my brother about how it's going with the Kittens & Claws club. I'm happy to announce that they have been racking in at least triple the investment that they put in from the beginning. With all of the new work that we've taken on, we need to find a way to clean this money. I am proposing that we open a second Kittens & Claws club here to take care of that for us." She looks around the room, ready to put it to a vote, but I don't see the need. We're all about the money, and we're all about the strip clubs. I think a new Kittens & Claws would be awesome here.

"Fuck yes, Boss!" Muffler says.

"You don't even have to ask," Abyss says. "I've been waiting to get back up there since the last time I went to go visit. The club is off the chain."

"All I wanna know is, can I take the first security detail," Mug says.

With that, we all laugh, and Boss calls the end of church. Just as I am gathering up my shit and am about to walk out, she calls out for me.

"Yeah, Boss?" The only reason she will be waiting until everyone else has left it's because she has a specific duty just for me. Even though I'm a full-patched member, sometimes it feels like I'm not doing enough. Boss needs me to do something. I am more than willing to get that shit done.

"I know you've been getting a little restless lately, so just checking in with you to see if you're up for taking a ride in a week or so. I want to make sure we secure a few or more liquor partnerships. It's a hassle getting them across sometimes, but the payout is astronomical." She tilts her head to the side and looks off as if she were thinking about the influx of cash.

"For sure. I'll get on it, say Thursday?" I want to stay around for a few days just to make sure everything is cool at the clubhouse.

"Yeah, that works fine." Boss nods her head, and just as she is about to say something else, my phone buzzes in my pocket.

"Shit." I fumble into my pocket and pull up my phone just to see it's my sister calling.

"Go and take it. That's all I have to say for now. We can talk later." Boss just messages me, and I answer the call.

"Well, look who finally realizes that they have my fucking number." I joke around with my sister, I know she tries to call me as much as she can, but with her job, she's always on the run. Also, I know she fucks with me just as badly as I am back with her.

"Hush, I knew I should've called someone else. You always getting on my nerves." She chuckles, and I hear some papers shuffling.

"Yeah, yeah. What's going on? Everything good with you?"

"For sure. I'm actually just calling to see if you are available today. I don't know if you had anything to do for the club." She heaves out a sigh, and I no longer hear the paper shuffling.

"I don't have anything planned. Want to tell me what you want?" I feel my eyebrows furrowing, and part of me is wondering if she has some type of favor that she's trying to ask me for.

"I mean nothing, really. I was just calling to see if you wanted to have dinner or something. Catch up."

"Catch up? That's all that you really want?" I stand with the phone to my ear, waiting for her to tell me the real reason why she wants to meet up with me.

"Ugh, always so annoying! You're right. Actually, I've been having a shit week, and I really just wanted somebody to vent to. Can't do it with anyone here at my job, so what are big brothers for?"

I hear a certain sadness in her voice, and although I know Beretta is strong and can take care of herself, as her brother, I always feel like I have to look out for her. If she needs somebody to talk to, no matter what it is about, I can be there for her.

"Yeah, let me know where you wanna meet." She tells me some ritzy Italian restaurant downtown.

The type where most of the people inside have on sports jackets. I want to bitch about the location, but I know she'll try to get out of meeting up if she thinks I don't want to go.

As we get off the phone, I head up to my room. I think about just showing up to the restaurant in some dirty jeans, boots, and a tank top under my cut. That will be one way to get us kicked out even faster. After thinking better of that decision, I pull out a pair of clean dark jeans, dark boots, and a black Henley. I'm not going to wear a tie or no shit like that, but at least I look presentable.

In the back of the closet, I see the only pair of dress pants that I own. I've never had a reason to wear them. I bought them back when Giada and I were still dating. Just in case we were to go some-place fancy. Now that I'm on my own, I won't wear any dress clothes if I don't need to. I never want to have to change who I am for anyone.

THE RIDE to the restaurant is actually pleasant. I take the time to clear my head and think about the next run I'm going to have to make for the club. When I pull up to the restaurant, the valet is quick to let me know that they don't park motorcycles. Part of me wants to just drive up on the fucking curb and leave it in front of the restaurant. I take a deep breath and park my bike on the corner past the restaurant and walk back.

When I get into the restaurant, I give my sister's name, and they usher me to a table. Instantly I feel eyes from every corner of the room on me. It's like they can tell I am bad news just from where they're sitting. I clench my jaw and do my best to ignore the blatant stares. A small mousy-looking waitress comes up to me, and I can see the fear on her face. Almost as if she thought just by coming over here to talk to me, I would hurt her.

"Good evening, sir. My name is Lisa. Will it just be you today?" Her voice is small, and I have to lean in to hear her well. I do my best to give her a polite smile and ease her discomfort.

"No, beautiful. I'll be waiting for my sister to get here. In the meantime, can I get a glass of water?" I make sure to keep my eyes on her's, and as I call her beautiful, I see a slight blush rise up on her face. Now the fear that was just there is replaced with giddiness.

Everyone loves a compliment.

She nods her head and quickly walks off to get my beverage.

I pull up my phone and see that I'm right on time. As usual, my sister is not. I swipe through my contacts looking for her number, and just as I hit call, I see her charging into the restaurant. She barely registers how everybody stares at her.

"I know, I know, I'm late." She sits on the chair opposite of me with a heavy puff of breath.

"Yeah, though only about 10 minutes. If you were here on time, I would think something serious was happening." I lean forward and look over my sister's face. She still looks the same, but I can see the stress building up on her features. I'm glad she's able to call on me to get whatever is bothering her off her chest.

"Do you know them? I'm surprised they let you in here like that." She raises one eyebrow and gestures with her chin to my cut.

"I wish a motherfucker would say something about my vest." I stare daggers at her, but it does nothing but make her laugh.

"Yeah, I know. Nobody's gonna come mess with the big bad hood rat." She bounces her head from side to side, and I'm making a gesture, and I pick up one of the complimentary bread rolls and flick a crumb add her.

"So, you got me here. Tell me what's going on." I lean forward, absolutely wrapped up in everything that she says. It doesn't take her long to get into why this week has been so difficult for her. I do my very best to remain calm and give her constructive advice. I try to be her place of Zen while she's so upset.

All of that shit goes out the window when I turn my head and see the one person I never wanted to see again.

Mr. Romano. Only known to me as my ex-girlfriend's father. The one who is so vehemently against his daughter and I being together. The same one who threatened to call the cops anytime I was near. The same one who told me his daughter didn't want to see me again.

"Hello! You still here with me?" Beretta squints and leans closer putting her elbows on the table. We've already been given our appetizers, so she has to move them away for her to make room. We haven't been here very long, so our entrées have not made it to us.

Unfortunately, I'm not sure I'll be able to contain the reasonable side of me long enough for us to get our food. Since she's been gone, I've periodically tried to look for her. Not necessarily to get her back or to curse her out for just leaving but more so just to lay eyes on her one last time. She left so suddenly that it almost felt like I was waiting for her to call. Like there's no fucking closure about the situation. Anytime I might have come across one of her parents to ask about her, they made it increasingly obvious that they would never help me get in contact with her. Hell, they never even fucking told me what college she went to. It was some huge fucking secret, and I was the only one not let in on it.

"I can't believe those motherfuckers are here." My voice is low, and I'm grabbing the edges of the table, trying to make myself stay in my seat. I don't want to embarrass my sister, and the last thing I need right now is this restaurant calling the cops on me because I make a scene.

"What are you talking about? Who is here?" My sister put her hand on mine, trying to get me to calm down. She knows when I'm at my edge.

"That asshole over there. That's Giada's father," I hiss out, and her face automatically drops. If anyone in the world knows how badly that girl messed me up, it's Beretta.

"Shit . . . I know this might be a stupid question, but even if you go over there now, do you think they would not tell you anything? Giada is grown. She can make decisions by herself. It seems sort of ridiculous to not let you know where she is simply because they don't like you. Why not let her make those decisions on her own." Beretta takes the napkin that's in her lap and throws it down on the table. She's getting just as pissed as I am.

I take a calming breath and wipe my hands on my jeans. The both of us can't be in here screaming. I may never want to come back to this restaurant again, but I'm sure my sister will. This is just her type of place.

That doesn't mean for one second, I'm not gonna go over there and ask them about Giada.

"I'm just gonna go over there and speak with them for one second." Before I have a chance to get up, Beretta's hand shoots out, and she grabs my wrist.

"Brother, I know this is always going to be a sore point for you, but try not to get in trouble, okay?" She stares at me with concern in her eyes.

I give her a tight smile and use my free hand to pat hers. I am old enough to be able to control myself now. Just because I want to take this man's face and break it over my knee doesn't mean I'll do it. Besides, there are too many witnesses.

Slowly, without bringing too much attention to myself, I grab one of the empty chairs at the table next to Mr. and Mrs. Romano. Before they have a chance to look up, I drag the chair to their table and sit down.

Just as Mr. Romano starts to tell me that this is a private dinner, I see his eyes widen once he gets a good look at my face. At least now I know he knows who I am.

"Get out of here. You're not welcome," Mr. Romano says through clenched teeth.

"I'm used to not being welcomed. That's never stopped me before." I look from him to his wife. I notice that his wife has yet to look me in the eyes. Not only is she looking down, but her hands are tightly clenched together. And her face looks ashen. I don't remember ever being too disrespectful to her, especially not enough for her to feel this fearful of me.

I focus my attention back on Mr. Romano. "I've actually just come over to say hello. And maybe to find out if you had any further information about Giada. I know she's out of school by now, so there is no reason I shouldn't be able to wish her well."

Mr. Romano leans in close, "Dante, I don't care if she's 80 years old and on her deathbed, I'm never going to tell you where she is. She doesn't want to see you." He makes sure to emphasize the last of his words, almost as if he were trying to drill them into my skull.

"Yeah, I've heard that. But if that's the case, she needs to tell me herself. Until she does, I'm not going to stop asking, and I'm not gonna fucking give up." I make sure to keep eye contact with him, but I don't see any fear, only determination. He may be just as hardheaded as I am.

It's only when Mrs. Romano sucks in a shuttered breath that I break out of my trance. "I hope you two have a wonderful evening," I say before I stand and walk back over to my sister.

When I sit back down at a table, Beretta exhales strongly. "Well, if no one is screaming, I guess that went better than it could have."

I want to laugh at her joke, but I'm so torn up inside, so pissed off that this is still having such an effect on me even after so many years.

Doing my best to ignore everything else around me, I finish meeting with my sister, and even though I can't give her the type of advice that I know she's looking for, I keep my ears open for her to be able to vent. Every few minutes, my eyes dart to the Romano table. I can't hear what they say, but it seems like the conversation is pretty heated. At one point, I see Mrs. Romano crying. Once they finish their meal, both Mr. and Mrs. Romano pay and get ready to leave. I keep my eyes glued on my sister mostly because I don't want the temptation of going after Mr. Romano. So, when he walks out the door, and I don't see his wife with him, I am curious as to where she's gone.

After just one sweep of my eyes, I see her walking toward the bathrooms. She came in through the side entrance. Before I can look away, she locks eyes with me. She doesn't say anything, but for the life of me, I swear I see her mouth the word come.

The male and female bathrooms are close together, so I go to the bathroom myself. Right before I make it to the bathroom, Mrs. Romano turns and starts walking back in the opposite direction as if she were going back to the car.

Just as I'm about to go into the men's room, Mrs. Romano grabs hold of my hand and slips me a paper. She doesn't say anything, not sorry, not help. She simply puts the paper in my hand and walks off.

I don't stop in the hallway. Instead, I continue into the bathroom. Whatever is on this paper, she obviously wants it to be kept a secret.

Just as I get to the mirror, I quickly open the

paper. It looks like it's been crumpled for a long time. On the small piece of paper is 'The DiGiovanni's'. I flip the paper over to see if there's anything else on the other side, but that's all there is.

I have no idea what this means, but I know something isn't right.

CHAPTER THREE

*G*IADA

It's not long before Luigi comes back. I know I shouldn't be happy that he's here, but something about having more than just the help around brings a little bit of joy. I've been here for so long that even the one person I never wanted to see again is something for me to get out of bed for. When he comes today, he brings candy. It's not like I can't tell the help to order candy for me, but for some reason, this means more.

"I wonder if you're in the mood to play a give a little get a little game today." Luigi takes a step forward closer into my space, and for some reason, even though he's been here a few times already, I have yet to get comfortable around him.

In fact, every time he's around, I feel more and more anxious. "What's it gonna cost me today?"

Luigi chuckles before he shows his hand in his pocket and looks around as if he's really trying to figure out what the cost will be. "It'll cost you holding my hand."

My eyebrows jumped up. I wonder what he's going to offer for that. So far, we haven't done any type of touching, and I would rather keep it that way. "What do I get in exchange?"

"I will let you come outside with me. We can't leave the property, but we can go past the garden."

I'm sure he knows that I'm not allowed to go past the garden. It's the only place on the estate where I can get any type of outdoor exercise. It still has a covering, so I'm not fully outside. I think about it for a while, and even though I'm jumping at the chance to spread my legs a little bit, I'm not too sure I feel safe being alone with Luigi.

"Come on, Giada, I promise I'll be a perfect gentleman." He gives me a charming smile, only the smile doesn't put me at ease. It bunches up the nerves in me tighter.

"Fine, I'll take a walk with you."

He waits for me while I put on something appropriate to wear outside, and just like he says, he holds my hand the entire time that we're walking. The feel of his hand against mine makes me want to crawl out of my own skin. He tries a little bit of small talk, and just to keep moving on, I indulge him.

There were a few times, I tried to pull my hand away, but every time I did, he tightened his grip even more. I don't like it. He squeezes too hard. I don't want to give him the satisfaction of complaining, but every time he does, I see a little smirk appear on his lips. He knows what he's doing. It's a power-play. He just wants me to know that he's the one in charge.

Once we get back to the estate, I figure he's just going to let me go back inside and go about his day. I'm surprised when he stops and turns me to face him.

I tried to pull away from him again, and this time he let my hand go. But it's only until he put one of his hands on my hip.

I look up into his face, and the bright sun is shining behind him. In this atmosphere, he almost looks handsome. I feel so conflicted. Out of all the time that I've been here, Luigi has been nicer to me in the last few days than anyone has been in the last decade.

When he lifts his hand and drags one finger down my cheek, I lean into it. It feels nice. It feels like someone actually cares about me. I don't know the last time someone made me feel like this.

I automatically think about just that. It was Hoodrat. He was the last one to make me feel like this. In fact, how Luigi is making me feel there's nothing but a very, very small compared to how Hoodrat used to make me feel.

I take a step back from Luigi and cross my arms over my chest. I know what it must feel like to suffer from Stockholm syndrome. I never want to like Luigi. I'm only feeling like this because there are no other options. It's because of him and the people that he works for, but I'm stuck here. It's because of them I don't have Hoodrat.

"I've done my part. I'd like to go back to my room now." I say it as harshly as I can to let him know that what we've done today means absolutely nothing to me. I don't know what type of game he's trying to play, but I'm not going to fall victim to it. I'm going to use him just as much as he uses me. If he is going to let me go outside just for holding my hand, that is all he'll get. We don't need to have small talk, and we definitely don't need to be friends.

We walk quickly to my room, and all the while, I make sure I don't make any eye contact with him. I don't want to prolong this any more than I already have. When I crack the doorknob and pull it open, Luigi tries to stop me.

"Giada, please don't make this harder than it has to be." His words are sinister, but the tone makes it sound like he's looking out for me.

"I'm going to make it hard. You and the rest of the people that are keeping me here have taken everything away for me. I'm not gonna make it easy for you to get away with it." I glare at him for one final second before I open my door and step inside, closing it in his face.

Suddenly, I realize there are no locks on the door. There's no way for me to call for help. Even though I was locked up here for so long, when I was in my room, I felt mostly safe. Now that I know he and anyone else can just walk in, I don't think I'm ever going to feel safe again.

CHAPTER FOUR

HOODRAT

Abyss, Muffler, and Reno all trail behind me as we blow through to the Finger Lakes. A few days after Boss asked me to set up a run to secure more liquor partnerships, we got word of a few wineries and distilleries up here that would be interested in giving a few wholesale deals for the club. Of course, they wanted to be listed as one of the sponsors.

The Kittens & Claws club is becoming a huge name up in Toronto, and everyone is trying to get a piece of the action that we've got going on up there. The ride is long, but it gives me a lot of time to think about what happened that day back at the restaurant.

I thought about trying to find Mrs. Romano and ask her what the note meant, but I figured that was a bad idea if she was doing it so her husband didn't find out. After I shot down that idea, I start to think about all the DiGiovanni families I know and even some I don't know personally. None of them have anything to do with Giada. The more I look into any of the DiGiovanni's I know about, the more frustrated I become.

I need more information. Mrs. Romano could be talking about any fucking body in the world.

"Hey man, I need to stretch my legs. I'm cramping up back here," Reno says, and I jerk back to attention. I almost forgot that the three of them were behind me. I'm so lost in my own fucking world.

"Shit, my bad. Yeah, let's pull over right here. It looks like there are a few good places to get something to eat as well." The four of us pull over, and I stay in the van as the others get up and walk around. I don't really have a strong desire to look around right now. My eyes roam over the street, and my gaze catches on a street sign. Memories and neurons start firing in my brain as I remember that one of the DiGiovanni's on my list just happens to have a restaurant up here. Not long after Giada went away, he basically up and moved up here. I thought it was odd, but I didn't think anything of it, but now that I'm here so close to one lead of many, I don't think I can sit back and just let it go. I don't bother to tell the others that I'm leaving. They all went separate ways anyway. I'm sure I'll be back before they finish eating. In the meantime, I can go check on Luigi DiGiovanni.

TODAY MUST BE my lucky day because I'll be damned if I don't find Luigi exactly where I thought he'd be and on his way out the door, to boot. I don't approach him since I don't want to spook him if I don't have to. Instead, I fall back and follow him when he jumps onto the road. He takes a winding road that leads out into a stretch of more secluded land. Something is off about him staying all the way out here. The last I heard, he didn't have any family or any big farm that he needed to fucking take care of, so what's with all the damn secrecy?

After another fifteen minutes of following him, my phone goes off, and I ignore it. I know it's the guys trying to figure out where the fuck I am. This is taking way longer than I expected. Right as I'm beginning to worry about gas, Luigi slows and turns onto a large strip of land. I wait until he's all the way in before I turn down the same way. There's a huge gate surrounding the entire perimeter, and on the inside is a huge house that can't be for just him.

What if Giada's in there? What if this is the place that her mother was talking about. It's definitely far away where no one would come looking for her, and it definitely looks like there's enough security.

My phone buzzes again, and this time I pick it up. I don't want the guys calling in the fucking cavalry because they can't find me.

"Hoodrat, what the fuck, bro? Where are you? We came back to look for you, and you were gone. We ate already. You straight?' Muffler asks, and I'm tempted to lie. These are my brothers. If there's anyone in the world who's going to help me with some off-the-wall shit like breaking into this high-security estate, it's them.

"I'm straight, I had to do a little surveillance, and I wound up tailing the mark a little too far. It'll take me a while to get back to you."

"Surveillance? Did you find what you were looking for?" Muffler asks, his voice serious.

"Not yet. I can't get in. He's in some super fortified, high-fenced castle shit, and I can't get through. I'm going to have to find a different way, but I didn't want this shit to get messy." I rub a hand over my face. That frustration I was feeling before simmers again right under the surface. I just want some fucking answers.

"You should try a drone," Muffler says as if it's the most obvious answer in the world.

"A drone?" I don't know shit about that. I wouldn't even know how to work one of those fragile pieces of shit.

"Yeah, that way, you can get over the fences and look for what you need to without tipping off anyone in security and without getting your hands dirty. This shit is all the fucking rage right now. Usually, the rich and the smart are the ones using it, though you have the dumbasses trying to get in on the drone action," he huffs out, and I shake my head.

"Whatever, man. You know where I can get one of those?"

"For sure, tell me where you're at, and we'll bring it to you. Either you want to do it early in the morning or later at night when it's not so obvious someone is peeping through the windows using a small remote-controlled electronic device." Muffler chuckles lightly, and even though I should be keeping a clear head, all I can think about is finding a way into that estate.

I don't know why I have such a bad fucking feeling about this, but I do. I just hope this drone will give me the answers I so desperately need.

GIADA

I pull the brush that Lu bought for me through my hair, and I love how easily it gets through my strands. Lu has been on his best behavior, and the more I try to force myself not to see him in a different light, the more I can't help it. He may be working with the people who are keeping me here, but he's the only one who has treated me this well. Maybe it's time I start focusing on something good instead of all the negative that's been going on over the past decade. Sure my life is nothing like I thought it would be, but I'm alive and well taken care of.

When I hear the downstairs door open and his familiar voice come floating up the stairs, I'm surprised at the influx of excitement I feel. There's a soft knock on my bedroom door, although it's already open. Lu is standing right at the threshold with a bag full of wonderful-smelling food and wine. "I was wondering if you'd be up for spending some time with me? Dinner?" he asks, and I nod with a gentle smile on my face.

"That smells absolutely divine," I tell him, and he seems to appreciate the praise.

He makes quick work of getting a nice little place setting arranged right here in my bedroom. We had a wonderful talk over the wine that he brought. We are basically cackling with hysterical laughter as I down my fourth glass of wine.

"Giada, I know we said that we were going to have some sort of deal in place, but I do hope you know that spending time with you is more than just part of the job for me. I'm so happy to hear you laughing right now." Lu reaches over tentatively and cups my cheek with his hand.

It's foreign, and I instinctually want to back away. But maybe this is exactly what I need. Perhaps I need to feel something different just to let me know that I'm still alive. I lean into his touch, and when I see him slowly move forward, I don't move away.

I want this. I want to feel.

Lu closes the distance and kisses me. Softly at first before he deepens it and pulls me out of my seat and into his lap. The feel of another person's body on mine breaks the dam that was holding my sexual frustration at bay. It's been years since I've been with anyone. Years since I've been with Dante, and my body is ready to break out of this drought.

"You're so beautiful," Lu says against my lips as he continues to grope and kiss me. I moan into his mouth, and he gets a better grip on me.

"I need you so bad, Giada." Lu humps up against my leg like a dog in heat, just slower. Maybe in a different circumstance, this would be hotter, but at best, it's lukewarm. I do my best to force every thought out of my mind, so I can focus on the feelings that he's giving me, but instead of going into a rolling boil of lust, I'm only at a soft simmer.

"I want you too, Lu," I say to encourage him and hopefully force my mind to stay present.

"Thank God," he grumbles as he picks me up with a struggling grunt and walks us over to the bed. He pulls off his shirt and opens his pants, all before he even touches me. When he does start working on my clothing, he starts humping against my leg again. I should be flattered that he's so turned on by me, but the more he does that, the more I want to cringe away. In a last-ditch effort, I close my eyes and let my imagination take over. In the darkness of my mind's eye, everything is marginally better.

I help him get my clothes off, and he begins to kiss me harder again. I shift my body over so one of his legs is in between mine. If he can use my thighs to get himself off, why can't I use his? I roll my hips, making sure to press down on his much wider leg. I get as much pressure as I can right where I need it the most, and slowly I feel my pussy getting wetter.

I hear words being spoken into my ear, and the hands on my skin somehow start to change.

"You hear me, baby?"

I gasp out but don't open my eyes. I know that voice . . . Dante. I grab hold of the body on top of me tighter, and I race to pull him up, so I can kiss his lips. My passion ramps up until I can't even remember how to breathe.

My head spins, and bright white lights flash behind my closed eyelids. I force myself to take in a few deep breaths as a warm mouth trails down from my lips to my breast. My back bows off the bed when I feel the heat enclose around it.

"Oh God," I moan, and Dante's familiar chuckle riles me up even further. He knows how much I love having my nipples played with. He spends only a small amount of time before he starts to shuffle my panties down off my legs. I don't bother to ask him about a condom. We never used one anyway.

"You're soaking wet," he says as he kisses his way back up my body.

"For you, always," I mutter, and I'm gifted another deep groan. God, I always love the way Dante makes me feel when we make love.

I hear the rip of foil and the bed dipping slightly as he positions himself over me, "I'm going to fuck you so hard." He grunts out, and I feel his cock head pressing into me, but something feels different. I feel the slightly unnatural pull of latex against flesh. I realize he's wearing a condom. I can't be bothered to ask him why once he starts to pump into me. Something still feels off. I move my body, trying to get into a comfortable position, but he's not hitting my spots like he normally does.

Even though it's not the best we've ever had, I'm so pent-up it doesn't take but a few strokes to get me to explode. My eyes spring open, and a bright light blinds me before an image of Dante's face appears right as I feel the first thunderous ripple of my orgasm take hold. My eyes slam shut again, and I ride it out, letting the pleasure pulse through me.

"Oh, yes, Dante," I moan loudly.

"What the fuck?"

My world stops along with my air.

My eyes pop back open again, and my hands fly to my throat. I claw at the hand pressing down on my neck, trying to get it off.

"What the fuck did you just call me bitch?"

My gaze comes back into focus, and I realize that it's not Dante over me but Luigi. I must have imagined that it was Dante I was fucking and not Lu. "Stop!" I try to speak, but his hand is so tight around my neck that I'm unable to get anything out.

I do my best to kick up, but that only reminds me that his cock is still inside of me.

"You fucking worthless bitch! I gave you more than anyone, and this is how you fucking repay me!" Lu pulls his hand back and brings it down with an incredible force right against my face. I kick again, now desperate to get him off me.

"This what you want, whore? Huh? You want me to be that worthless piece of shit, Dante? The lowlife scum?" He grabs my hair hard and tilts my head far to the side with enough force that I'm screaming in agony as he cruelly begins to pump inside of me again. There's no rhythm or care about my pleasure. He's just blindly stabbing inside of me. All the while, he uses his other hand to continue to beat on me.

It hurts. Everywhere.

Bucking my body as hard as I can, I am able to dislodge him from inside of me, but that doesn't stop the blows from his fist from raining down on me. Even curled up into a small ball, Lu still manages to land quite a few punches. I mistakenly turned my head the wrong way, and Lu hits me again, but this time I feel a sickening crunch in my nose, and blood pours down my face.

"You nasty bitch. What the fuck do I want with you now?" He mushes my face one more time before he climbs off the bed, leaving me there. I'm in so much shock and pain I can't even cry. My eyes follow Lu while he quickly puts his clothes back on, the condom still on his dick when he pulls his pants up. He walks over to the romantic setup of the food he brought for us to share and picks up some of the leftovers with his hand.

"Here." He throws what he has on the floor. "Since you want to act like such a fucking dirty dog, you can eat like one too." He glares at me for another second before he leaves my room like nothing amiss ever happened.

I roll out of bed and, doing my best to ignore the pain, rush over to the door and shove a chair under the knob to lock it. That's the only security I have.

Lu could come back at any moment and decide he's not done with me. Someone else could. Now that he's started, I'm sure there's going to be more pain. I can't deal with this. I have to get out. This is hell, pure and simple.

I stumble back to the bed, where I wrap my arms around my naked, bloody and battered body. The cries that leave my mouth come from the depths of my soul. My life is a fucking nightmare, and all I want to do is wake up.

CHAPTER SIX

HOODRAT

I wait patiently for them to get to the meeting point that I give the boys. Since I have the van, they have to take a cab to where I am. It's an expense but not as bad if I had to waste time by going all the way back there only to come straight here again. Instead of setting up in front of the large estate, I have Muffler, and the rest of them meet me at a small motel. That way, we can wait until nightfall before we go back and use the drone.

"You sure you know how to use this shit?" I ask Muffler.

"Yeah, man, it's not that hard. Just like playing a video game, except this game is an expensive piece of equipment, and the video feed you're looking at is real life. Besides that, it's all the same." Muffler shrugs his shoulders as he flips the power switch to figure out how charged the machine already is.

"Whatever, as long as you know what you're doing, I don't really care." I drop down on the rickety bed and drop my head into my hands. I should give Boss a call and let her know what's going on, but I'm really fucking scared that she's just going to tell me to finish what I'm supposed to be doing. How the fuck can I be thinking about doing more for the club when I can't even stay on task?

"I know you said you were doing some surveillance, but do you want to tell us what it is exactly that you're looking for? No matter what it is, we'll help you, but it might help to know what the fuck has got you looking like that." He points at me, and I glare at him. I don't know what I look like, but I'm sure it's not good. All these years living with the idea that Giada up and left me simply because her family didn't think I was a good fit, only to find out now that maybe that wasn't the case. I thought I loved that girl. But if I truly loved Giada the way I thought I did, why didn't I fight for her harder? I don't know what the fuck to believe, but I know now that I'm getting close to something I can't fucking give up, not again.

"I'm looking for my ex . . . my woman . . . my . . . fuck man, I'm looking for Giada." I push my hands in my hair and tug at the same time. I start bouncing my leg fast. It feels like I'm not moving fast enough, but everything is speeding by.

"Shit, you for real?" Abyss asks.

"Yeah. I saw her parents the other day when I went to go meet my sister. I thought it was the same bullshit as normal, but then her mother slipped me a fucking note that pointed me in the direction of the DiGiovanni's. There's no other info, and I know a few dozen DiGiovanni's. I don't even know if this one is the right one. I'm fucking searching for a needle in a goddamn haystack," I exclaim, and now I have all three of their attention.

"Fuck, bro, that shit's tough. You know Boss will put everyone on this, though. If this isn't what you're looking for, she'll make sure to put everything on it until we find out for sure what's going on with Giada," Reno says.

I nod my head but don't bother to speak anymore on the subject. I don't necessarily need them to know that even if we do find her, there may be a way she doesn't want to be with me anyway. I could be pulling her out of a place where she's been happy the last decade.

I slip back into my own mind as we wait for it to get darker and for the drone to fully charge. Once all that is done, we make our way back to the estate and set up a semi-decent task list.

We need to count the staff and the cars, search for any weaknesses for access, and most importantly, we need to try and locate Giada. Muffler activates the drone, and within a few seconds, the small machine is floating nearly silent in the air above. I check his phone, which has a direct link to the video feed. I can see above the trees and the fence now. I'm really fucking impressed that he had such a good idea.

"Get higher," I order, and he controls the drone pushing it further up, so we have an eagle-eye view of the property. From what I can see, the fence wraps all the way around except for a long stone wall that cuts through the trees. It probably was part of the original architecture but was mostly replaced as the years went on. At least that's the best guess I can come up with. It also looks like it might be the only place where I might be able to sneak in. It'll be a tight squeeze, but if I can knock down part of the wall, I'd be able to get in.

"Do you see any cars there?" Reno asks, and I search around the actual property to see what else I can make out. I do see three cars toward the rear of the facility but no others.

What's more confusing to me is I don't see any guards. "Only the three, but I don't see any security on the grounds."

"That doesn't mean they aren't there. That just means we can't see them," Muffler says, and I take a deep breath trying to keep my cool. I can't afford to make any mistakes right now.

"Can you get us closer to the windows, or do you think whoever's inside will see?" Reno asks.

"I can, most of the time, people don't even realize a drone is around, and if someone turns, I'll just fly it away," Muffler replies very confidently.

Abyss, Reno, and I huddle closer to Muffler as he flies down to the upper level of the building and starts looking in the windows. The few that are clear for us to look into that is. We see one woman so far that looks to be a housemaid of some kind. She's vacuuming and moving things around. Another two windows that we look into show us that there's no one in them. Everything inside looks very ornate.

Very high class, but it's not out of the ordinary based on what I'm seeing from the outside.

We scan through another few rooms and then the back side of the house. I don't see anyone I know, not even Luigi. It's all starting to feel like a dead end.

"Shit! We got movement over here," Abyss says, and I turn to see where he's looking, only to see the same car that I'd followed all the way out here racing away from the property. Our truck is far enough behind some brush that I'm hoping Luigi didn't see it, but I can't be certain. With my breath held, I wait to see if he stops, but once he continues around the corner toward the main road, I feel like we're in the clear.

"Oh, what the hell is this?" Muffler mutters, and I turn back toward him to see what he's looking at. Everything was dead a few seconds ago, but now it seems like in a blink of an eye, a bunch of shit is happening.

"What?"

"That window is open now," he says, and we all bend to see what he's talking about. The drone tilts down, and I see something that looks like a cord or long cloth dangling out of the window.

"What the hell is that?" I lean as close as I can get, so I can see the screen as he flies the drone down a bit more. This time we can see directly into the room. My legs feel like they are sinking into the dirt. A woman moving frantically with long dark hair comes into view.

I know those curves. I know that hair. That's fucking Giada.

"Holy shit, is she going to jump from there. That's way too fucking high."

"No! Fuck! That's her! I have to go! Move!" I jump up and make a mad dash for the side of the estate that has the stone wall. I'll break that shit down with my fists if I have to.

Abyss tackles me to the ground before I can get any closer. Muffler and Reno are on me too.

"Hood! We can't go in! We need to wait for fucking backup! We can't!" Abyss hisses out near my ear, but I fight to get him off.

"No, fuck that! She's fucking in there. I need to go!" I bark back and try to push back up again.

"Hoodrat, if you run in there now, they're going to know she's trying to escape. You're going to get her fucking killed, man," Muffler says, and that gives me pause.

She's not expecting me to be here. She's trying to make a run for it, and so far, besides the fact she's about to jump from a height that'll surely break some fucking bones, no one is any wiser. If I go in guns blazing, she'll get caught.

They're right. I can't do anything right now besides wait for backup or see if she makes it out on her own. Once again, I have to wait to see if my woman comes to me.

CHAPTER SEVEN

GIADA

My chest hurts not only from the rate at which I'm breathing but also from the residual pain left from the beating I took. I have to get out of here. There's no other way for me, and I see that now. Whatever I do, I have to do it quickly. There are cameras in the house, so I know once I start moving around, the guards are going to see me. The only way that I can see this working is if I jump from the window. The only problem with that idea is I'm up on the third floor. If I jump from this height, I might not die, but I'm not going to be able to get away either. I thought that I'd get some sheets together, but there's never any extra bedding, and what's here isn't enough to get me down three flights

Then on top of that, right beneath my window is a dip for water runoff. No matter how I look at it, I'm going to be hurting when I hit the ground. Still, I have to give it a try. If I die, so be it. The option of staying here even one more fucking day is abhorrent.

As soon as I hear the door downstairs open and shut, letting me know that Luigi is truly gone for the day, I grab my sheets and everything else that I can find. I tried to get the drapes, but I couldn't get them down. With all the sheets and the extra clothing that I had here, the makeshift rope takes me to about the middle of the second floor, at least that's what I'm thinking. I hope it's not shorter than that. I'm sure that I can make a jump from the second floor.

I put my sneakers on and some pants that I was allowed to have, and I quickly tied the fabric to one end of the heating pipes in the room. It's the only structure I know that is strong enough to hold me. The minute I push open those doors, the alarm will go off, and I'm not going to have long before the security is here. If I'm going to do this, I need to do it now.

Making sure to leave the chair wedged against the door, I take in a few deep breaths and grab one of the light fixtures off the wall. I have to pull hard to unmount it, but I'm happy when it comes off the wall in my hands, mostly intact. With the heavy item in my hand, I run over to the window but think better of just ramming it through the glass. It's a better chance that I'd hurt myself doing that before I even have a chance to get out of the window.

Instead, I wedge the metal fixture under the locking mechanism and pull with all the strength I have. The window creaks and groans, but nothing happens. After trying to get this thing to budge for about five minutes, it finally gives way, and I'm able to open the windows freely without any noise or broken glass. Unfortunately, out of the corner of my eye, I can see the dull pulsing red light going off. Someone will be here soon. Time to move.

I toss the fabric out of the window and shimmy myself over the ledge. My arms are already shaking before I even have a chance to get a good footing. I dare to take one peek down, and I want to throw up everything I've eaten. It's so high up. I have to push my fear away, so I scale down the side of the wall, moving fast but making sure I'm as safe as I can be. When I get to the edge of the makeshift rope, I look down to see I'm right below the second-floor window. The drop is still so much farther than I thought.

I don't have a choice now. I can't go back up. I say a quick prayer, close my eyes and let go.

Air rushes by my ears for what seems like an eternity, and then mind-numbing pain.

My lungs seize up for a moment as my body tries to adjust to what it is that I'm feeling. Once I do, I scream out in agony. My ankle is fucked up. It's almost my worst fear come to life. I didn't die, but there's no way I'm going to be able to run now.

I bite down on my lips to keep myself from screaming out any longer while I run my hands along my body to see if I have any other broken bones. When nothing jumps out as injured, I push myself up on the one good foot that I have and try to pull myself out of the ditch I fell in. I've only been along the back half of the estate, so I'm not really sure how to get out, but I take a chance and hobble toward the left.

I don't see anyone rushing out of the house, but I'm not going to take that chance. My leg buckles under me a few times, but I stay on my feet. As I turn to duck near the tree line by the side of the house, I see a long stone wall that I've gotten close to before. I can use that to help me move. Leaning against it, I hop quicker until, out of nowhere, one of the groundskeepers appears.

He has a shovel in his hand, and his eyes go wide when he sees me. Both of us stare at each other without moving until he blinks a few times and raises the shovel above his head.

"I don't know what you're doing out here or how you even got out, but you best get back up to your room now, or there's going to be fucking trouble," he snaps at me.

My eyes burn from the sweat pouring into them. I have nothing that I can use to defend myself. I'm just going to have to find a way to disarm him. I see something in back of him moving over the top of the stone wall.

Shit, there's more of them. I'm so fucking screwed!

"Please, just let me go. Please," I beg now, the tears strolling down my cheeks in hot rivulets.

"You know I can't do that. Get on back upstairs," the groundskeeper says and takes a step forward, but I don't move. I guess now is when he'll kill me.

I hear a clicking sound, and at the same time, so does the groundskeeper. He raises the shovel higher, but before he can turn around, the person behind him says, "Don't fuck around, old man." The next second I see the glint of a metal gun swiping through the air as whoever is behind him brings the butt of the weapon down on the groundskeeper's head.

I slide a step backward in shock when the body crumbles in front of me. The shock only intensifies when I look back up and see Dante.

"Giada, can you run?" he asks me.

I must have died when I fell from the window. That's the only explanation for how this is even possible. The imaginary Dante takes a step toward me, but I'm so scared I can't even move back myself.

"Giada, can you hear me? Can you run?" he asks again. This time his voice is laced with intensity.

The sound of a door slamming open somewhere in the distance breaks me out of my trance. I turn my head toward it and then back to Dante, who is still there waiting for me to say or do anything.

"No, I messed my ankle up."

His eyes drop down to my leg, "Fuck, okay. Come on." He turns and squats slightly.

"What?"

"Up on my back, we don't have time. We need to move right now." He waves his hand, trying to get me to hurry up. I use my good leg and hop as high as I can on his back, and he takes off toward the back end of the stone wall through the trees.

Everything is happening so fast I barely have

time to process it all. In fact, all I can think about is how I'm sure I'm going to wake up at any second. When Dante accidentally bumps my leg against the tree and a fresh wave of pain rockets through my body, I finally am able to believe that maybe I really am awake and this is real.

"How are you here? When did you get here? What's going on?" I ask him.

"We can't talk right now. I need to get you out of here first," he grunts out over his shoulder just as we get to a lower part of the stone wall. There's another man on the ledge with his hand reaching down.

"Go." Dante orders, and I reach up. The man heaves me over the stone wall before he reaches down and does the same for Dante. There's another man on the other side of the wall that helps me down, and then we are all getting into a small van.

"Shit! What the fuck just happened? I didn't see anyone else behind her. What about the other security?" the man who's now in the driver's seat says.

"They're downstairs or trying to get into my room. I wedged it shut," I answer with a trembling voice.

The van starts up, and we take off toward the main road. Is this really happening? Did I make it out?

Just as I'm about to ask, I see the same Rolls Royce that I've come to know so well. It's Lu's. With a squeak, I duck down to stay out of view and grab hold of Dante's leg. He looks down at me, and I finally look up at him. I'm safe.

I think I'm safe.

CHAPTER EIGHT

HOODRAT

When I saw Giada running toward me, even if she didn't know that I was there, I just couldn't stand by and let that man get in her way. Going against everyone's advice, I hopped over the stone wall and got Giada out of there. From the moment she looked up at me, it was like she's been in a trance. She's barely said a word to me as we race back toward the clubhouse, and part of me is worried that they might've done something to her mentally.

I've heard about people using electroshock therapy on people they keep enslaved. Every time I try to touch her, she cringes away, and I end up apologizing. Finally, after driving like a fucking maniac, we're almost home. Giada went to sleep about an hour ago and in all that time . . . all I could do was just *look* at her. I can't believe she's right here in front of me. After all these years apart, we've finally been reunited.

I also can't believe Luigi didn't follow us. When the car passed us, I thought for sure he'd have guessed we were the ones that had Giada, but he made no attempt to come for us. He'll be a problem for a different day. Right now, all I care about is getting Giada the help that she needs. And making sure Boss doesn't kick my ass out for doing this shit without her knowledge. I'm hoping with Muffler and Abyss to back me up, she'll see that I was either temporarily out of my mind or simply had no other choice.

"Do you want to call her parents or something?' Reno asks, looking over his shoulder at me.

"No. Not yet. I don't know if they had anything to do with this. If they did, I'd be paying them a separate visit," I grit out.

"I hear that," Abyss says. "This is crazy. Are you telling us that she's been up there the entire time? It's been years, right?"

"Yeah. Years. I left her up there for fucking years."

"Don't you fucking dare do that shit. You had no idea she was up there. If you did, you'd have broken down that fucking fence years ago. Don't put this on yourself. It's not going to do nothing but fuck you up emotionally," Muffler says.

"It's not your fault," a soft voice says, and I turn my head back to Giada. She's woken up and is staring at me again.

"G, I'm sorry. I didn't realize we were talking so loudly. You can go back to sleep if you want." I give her a smile but don't touch her.

"I can't, bad dreams," she replies, and I bite down on my tongue. "Everywhere I go, awake or asleep, there are bad dreams." A tear rolls down her cheek, and I fist my hands against my legs to keep from wiping it off.

"No more bad dreams, Giada. You're okay now. It's all going to be okay," I promise her, but I can't be totally sure that I'm telling her the truth. I'm not sure what she's into, but there may be a chance that we're in over our heads here.

***

We pull up in front of the clubhouse, and the guys rush in before me while I gather Giada in my arms. She lets me pick her up only because her ankle is in much worse shape now that all the adrenaline has worn off.

She's so light, and even in my grasp, she doesn't

stop looking at me. I love the feel of her in my arms, but I can sense how broken she is by her stare. What have they done to my girl?

"What in the fuck is this?" Boss curses out when I walk in the door. Everyone else is staring at the woman in my arms and us.

"I can explain," I try to say, and Boss storms over to me. The closer she gets, the more frantic Giada gets in my arms as if she's trying to crawl away. A low keening squeal comes out of her mouth, and the slight tremor she had moments ago has turned into full-blown shaking.

"Please, please, please," she begs, and Boss stops in her tracks, looking down at the woman in my arms.

I grip Giada closer to me but address Boss, "I can explain. Please, just let me put her down, and I'll come right back out and let you know what's going on." I look at my president and pray that she can see the need in my eyes. This isn't just me trying to bring some random woman into the clubhouse. This is Giada. She used to be the only reason for keeping me out of jail.

"Yeah, get her set up. Faith, Iris, you two go with him. Help him make sure our guest has everything she needs. Once she's calm, come back out here, and we're going to have that fuckin' talk." Boss glares at me for a second before she turns and lets the four of us walk over to my room.

I lay Giada down on the bed, careful of her leg. As I hover over her, I can see more cuts and bruises on her face and body. And finally, a handprint wrapped around her neck. This is fresh, like today fresh.

"He did this to you? Luigi did this?" I ask her, but she doesn't answer me. She just stares at me again.

"Hoodrat, not now," Faith says from behind me. When I turn to look at her, she's shaking her head.

I let Giada lay back, and I turn to talk to Faith, "I need to get these answers."

"I'm sure you do, but right now, that girl is still in the fight of her life. Maybe not physically, but mentally. She doesn't need you hovering over her, badgering her. When she's ready to be interrogated, you'll know. I'm assuming you brought her here because you wanted to help her, am I right?"

I look away and shove my hands in my pockets, letting out a hard sigh, "Of course, I want to help her."

"Okay, then listen to me. She needs rest, food, someone to look over her injuries, and most of all, just someone to be patient with her. Don't push her before she's ready," Faith says, keeping her voice soft.

"Yeah, you're right. I know you are. I'm sorry," I mutter.

"You don't need to apologize to me. I know you're in kick-ass mode. I just didn't want you to do something that would hurt her worse in the long run." Faith shrugs and kneels next to Iris in front of Giada.

I stay there for a while and help the girls get Giada what she needs. When it's time for her to shower, I stay by the door to give her some privacy, so she doesn't have to worry about me. I don't go far, but I give her space as she needs it.

About two hours later is when things finally calmed down, and the girls convinced her to eat some soup. I figure it's time I pay the piper and get on with my conversation with Boss.

When I come out, I'm happy to see the main area is pretty clear. I walk over to the stairwell, head up to the next level and go to her office door, then knock.

"Yeah, come on in," she calls out, and I step inside.

When she sees it's me, her face falls, and I watch her clench her jaw. "It's obvious that whoever that girl is, she means something to you, but right now, I'm feeling like maybe you've been keeping some important information. Firstly, I want you to tell me who did this to her."

I take a step closer to her, "Luigi DiGiovanni."

"Who is she?"

"Her name is Giada. She's my . . . she *was* my woman. We broke up years ago, or I thought we had when she vanished to go to college without telling me. Now I'm thinkin' that might not have been the case." I fist my hands at my sides, not wanting to be aggressive toward my president at all, but still feeling the boiling rage inside of me.

"Jesus. What about this Luigi? Does he know it was you that took her? Do we need to be worried about a fucking body popping up somewhere?" Boss stands up.

"No, I didn't get a chance to kill him . . . yet. He doesn't know it was me as far as I know."

Boss looks to the other side before she lets her arms down and looks back at me, "You know we're not going to let you go after this guy on your own. We're here for you, but you're going to have to keep me in the fuckin' loop. If I don't know what the hell is going on, we can't stay on top of this."

"You got it," I answer right away.

"Good, now, since you're all back here so early, I'm assuming our business with the liquor retailer went a little off the rails.

"Yeah, we didn't get it done. I can . . ."

She puts her hand up and waves away anything that I'm going to say, "You can stay right the hell here and take care of your woman."

"Thank you, Boss. I can't let them hurt her anymore," I say, admitting what I know is in my mind.

"We're going to help you make sure they don't." She nods once, and I walk out and back to my room.

Giada is in my bed, sleeping comfortably, and I have to do a double take when I close the door.

How many times have I imagined this very scenario? How many times have I wished for her to come back to me? None of this seems real, but even if this is a dream, I definitely don't want to wake up.

CHAPTER NINE

GIADA

Darkness surrounds me, and I can't see the bright lights on the ceiling. Where the hell has Luigi taken me now? I have to get out of here. I have to get out of here right now!

"Please, let me out! Help me!" I scream at the top of my lungs when a set of hands wraps around my shoulders.

"Giada! Wake up! You're okay. Listen to me, you're okay! It's me! Dante." The man says, and then one of his hands lets go of me, and the room is flooded with light. I have to blink a few times to get my eyes to focus. I do, and instead of Luigi, the first person I see *is* Dante. This *is* real. I *really* made it out. I collapse into his arms and cry my eyes out. I vaguely hear the sound of a door opening and closing.

"It's fine. Get out," Dante hisses over my head, but I don't bother to look up. Whatever the problem is, I know he's going to take care of it.

"Oh, God. I'm so scared. I'm scared," I say over and over into his chest. He rubs my hair and rocks me, trying to soothe me.

"It's over now. You're okay."

After a long while, I manage to get myself under control. "I'm sorry. I thought I was back at the house. I thought I was back with . . ." I let my voice trail off, and I close my eyes, trying to get the pictures of Luigi hovering above me out of my head. I don't want to feel him on my body, but everything I do seems to bring me right back to that moment. I feel the tears start to build up in my eyes again, and suddenly everything in the room starts to feel so hot. The women who were here before made sure to give me something that I thought would be comfortable to sleep in, but now it feels like it's burning my skin. I pull at the fabric, but Dante grabs my hand and stops me from doing that.

"Hey, what do you need? Tell me what's going on. Let me help you, G."

"I'm hot. It's so hot in here. I want to get it off. I

need to cool off." I talk, and even though in my mind I can say what I want clearly and fluently when I hear the words coming out of my mouth, it sounds like I'm hiccupping and hyperventilating. I don't know what's wrong with me right now.

"I feel like I can't breathe," I tell him, and I grab hold of his arm.

"You're having a panic attack. I'm going to help you. Do you want another shower? That'll cool you down," he says, looking into my eyes, and I nod my head quickly. That sounds like heaven right now. I swing my legs over the edge of the bed and try to stand, but I crumple right away. I completely forgot about my ankle.

"Shit, maybe we need to get you to the hospital so they can get a good look at that leg." He helps me back onto the bed.

"No, please. No hospitals. Luigi might not be here right now or even know where we are, but he has people all over the place. I don't even know how many. I don't want to go to the hospital only to have them find me and take me back. I can't go back there, Dante. You don't know what I've been through. Please, no hospitals," I explain to him, and he nods his head tightly.

"Okay, I hear you, Giada. I won't force you to do

anything you don't want to do, but we need to figure out a way to get this leg looked at." He breathes hard through his nose before he gets closer to my body, "If you still want that shower, I'm going to have to carry you. Is that okay?"

"Yes," I squeak out. I need the shower more than anything else. I need to have this burning feeling that's crossing my skin gone.

His big arms reach down and pick me up ever so gently. It doesn't even feel like we're moving, but I know we are when he gets me into the bathroom. He sits me down on the toilet and starts to reach for my clothing, but I don't want him to touch me. Not yet. I can't handle it right now.

"I can do it," I tell him, pulling my shirt down tight against my body.

"Giada, you know I'd never hurt you, right? I'd never . . ." He closes his mouth, and I wish there was a way for me to reach through all the mess in my mind so I could comfort him in some way. I heard what he was saying to the guys in the van about feeling like he's somehow to blame for all this happening to me.

"Giada, what happened?" he asks again, his voice is soft, and I want with everything I am to just let him know everything that I went through from the time that I was first kidnapped to the moment I ran into him on the back lawn of my high-priced prison. Yet even as I open my mouth to say something, nothing comes out. There's only pain and disgust.

"Dante, I can't. Not yet." I look away, thinking he's going to be mad at me, but he instead lifts my head, so my eyes are level with his.

"Giada, I'm here whenever you need to talk. Don't think that you have to rush for me. I just want to know how to help you. Tell me, and I'll do it."

"Let me take a shower. Do you have something so I can sit? I can't stand in there, and I don't think I'm comfortable yet with you watching me. I need some time alone." He nods his head and walks out of the bathroom for a second before he comes back with a small folding stool, something that you'd see people using outdoors. He sets it up in the shower and goes to leave me alone, just as I had asked.

"Dante," I call for him.

"Yeah, G?"

"Can you stay close, please? Just don't go away?" I don't want him to go too far because he's the only person I can trust. I don't know how to explain everything that's going on in my head right now. I don't want him gone, even though it almost actually hurts me to have him touch me physically.

"Don't worry, I'll be just right outside this door. I'm not going anywhere. You never have to worry about me leaving you again."

I nod, and he walks out of the bathroom, leaving me to take care of my needs on my own, exactly as I asked him. He said he'd be right outside, but I hope he doesn't hear me because there's no way I'm not going to be able to keep from breaking down in here. I can already feel the growing despair in the pit of my stomach. Being free had somehow caused me to be more afraid than when I was stuck in that room.

I don't know if it's because I know Luigi and whoever else he works for will be coming after me or because I know that I can't be with Dante again without bringing him problems that will get him into trouble. I think I'm the most afraid of the possibility that I could get used to life on the outside again. Outside of the prison, that was my life, only to have them show up in the middle of the night and take me right back. It's the fear of not knowing what's going to happen that really has me on edge.

I just sit here in the shower and let the water run down my face. I was strong enough to get out of that wretched place, but now I don't know if I'm strong enough to survive being free.

CHAPTER TEN

HOODRAT

The sound of Giada crying cuts me to the fucking core. I want to break down that door and pull her into my arms, but the words Faith told me earlier are still ringing in my mind. I thought for sure that I'd be able to keep my wits about me. That I'd be able to keep calm, but the longer she's hurting, the more I want to just rip someone's head off.

I know I told her I wouldn't be far, and I'm not, but I can't stand out here and just listen to her cry. I take a minute to gather myself before I walk out to the main area and hopefully get myself a drink. There are a few people still awake, and it seems like everyone is talking about me because when I walk into the room, everyone goes quiet.

"Who the hell died?" I grumble out.

"No one. Unless you're about to tell us all some bad news?" Faith says.

I know it's meant as a joke, but just thinking about Giada dying is enough to make me cringe.

"No, she's okay," I grumble and make my way to the very end of the bar. Not that it meant any different because Ricochet came over to talk to me. I don't typically mind what the rest of my club brothers and sisters have to say, but right now, I don't think any of them know what the hell I'm going through. How many of them can say that they left the love of their lives in the enemy's hands for over a decade? None.

"Bro, I'm not going to ask if you're good 'cause I know you're not, but how is she doin' in there?" Ricochet asks.

"She's a wreck. She's crying and can't bear for anyone to touch her. She woke up screaming a few minutes ago because she thought she was back there. She says she has nightmares. She's in the shower right now, but when I left, I saw some of her bruises. Someone did a fucking number on her today. I don't know about before, but I'm sure it was more of the same. She won't tell me what's going on, and it feels like everything I do is just a reason for her to push me away. I don't know what the fuck I'm doing." I reach over the bar and pull out the first thing my hand touches. Whiskey.

That'll do just fine.

"I know it, man. This shit is fucked. All you can do is just take it one day at a time, but in the meantime, maybe you can work on getting her some help," Ricochet says, and I'm just about to start talking when he puts his hand up, "I mean some professional help brother. Or if not, maybe she'll want to talk to Venom? That might be good for her to have someone else that's gone through some fucked up shit to talk to?"

I shake my head, and my first instinct is to tell him that it's not going to work. None of them understand what she's going through, but then on the same note, I can't just leave her emotional wellbeing to me. I've never been really good at that stuff, which was okay before, especially since I grew up with Beretta. If I could take all Giada's pain away right now, I would. The kicker is I don't even know where to start. Venom might be a good person for her to talk to. She's had some intense shit happen in her past as well.

If she'd only give me a target, I could take them out with no problem. But so far, Giada has yet to be able to tell me much more than she's scared. Though I can't blame her for that. If I were in her shoes, I'd be scared too.

"I don't know how much it'll help, but if she wants to do it and Venom is open to it, then I'll set it up. I think if she does get some of this shit out, it'll do wonders for her. I just don't think she's going to want to do that anytime soon. So far, she hasn't been able to tell me anything." I shrug, and he nods.

"Yeah, trying to get her to talk might take some time. The only thing that I can suggest is that you're patient with her. I know that's not something you want to hear right now, but this is going to be a long process any way you look at it. If she's as messed up as you're making it sound, it might be years before you get everything out of her."

I gasp and drop the bottle of whiskey in my hand. Years? "Fuckin' hell. She's going to be hurting like this for that long?"

"No, not like this. She'll always hurt, but it'll get better. She's a strong woman. If she's made it this long, then I'm sure she's going to come out on the other side stronger for it. Right now, it's an acute hurt. She's fresh out, and all she's probably thinking about is she's got to get away, even if she's already out of that damn place. She's thinking about how she's going to stay out. How she's going to make sure there's no more pain. You're going to have to let her go through that and just be there to support her."

I let my head fall to the bar and just think about everything he's telling me. I have no problem being there to support her, but I don't know if I can stand back and let her hurt. That's probably going to be the hardest part for me. How do I get through that? How do I sit by while she hides from me and cries herself to sleep?

A door opens from the side. "Hoodrat, you wrecked?" I hear Boss say.

I pop my head up and look at her, keeping my eyes glued to hers. "I'm straight. You need me?"

"Yeah, I wanted to find out if you had any more information. Something about how you got out isn't sitting right with me. I need to know what kind of implications this is going to have on the club, so we can be ready. I mean, they had this girl for over a decade, so there's no way they're just going to let her walk. I know you told me already that you didn't kill anyone, but what about witnesses? How did you figure out she was in there in the first place?"

I realize I never told her about the drone incident. "Actually, I went off on my own to track Luigi, but when I got there, the fence kept me from getting any further into the building. So, Muffler, in all his wonderful wisdom, suggested that I could use a drone to see what was going on where I couldn't go. It's a pretty cool device and allowed me to get eyes on her without anyone seeing us."

Boss chuckles quickly before she asks, "A drone, huh? Well, that's new. What about after, when you got her? Did anyone see you then?"

"No, while we were using the drone, we saw her climbing out of the window, more so jumping out of the window. She hit the ground and tried to make it out on her own, but she was stopped by the groundskeeper. I jumped over just as he was about to take her out, and I took him down instead. No one else was there to see us. According to Giada, they were all inside trying to get inside of her room."

She nods, "And what about getting away?"

"We were in the van and not the bikes. Luigi did drive by us when we got to the main road, but he was speeding back toward the estate. No one saw us. I'm sure our getaway was clean," I say with the most confidence. If there was anyone who saw us, I don't see how they would tie us back to the club.

"All right, I haven't heard anything about this from anyone. Since there's no chatter about it, maybe you guys did watch your asses good enough that there's not going to be any blowback. What about Giada? Did she say anything more?"

"I'm sorry, I haven't been very helpful," a small voice says from behind me.

Shit!

I turn and see Giada coming down the stairs. She's dressed in my clothes, and even from here, I can see in her eyes that she's lost. I just want my girl back, but I think that'll take a while. As long as I can see the light in her eyes again one day, it'll all be worth it.

CHAPTER ELEVEN

GIADA

"G, what are you doing coming down the stairs? I told you I'd be right here. You're going to hurt yourself." Dante comes rushing up to me as I try to hobble down the stairs. He did tell me he wasn't going to go far, but when I came out of the bathroom and didn't see anyone, I thought maybe he had changed his mind and left.

I'd have changed my mind, too, if I had to deal with some weeping person in my shower.

"You shouldn't be walking on that leg. Have you thought about going to the hospital? You may need to get it looked at," Boss says, coming up behind him.

"No, we're not going to the hospital. We'll take care of it in-house," Dante answers for me. He already knows how I feel about the hospital, so I'm happy he's taking what I'm telling him seriously.

"All right, I hear you." Boss turns and looks at me, "What about you? Besides the leg, how are you doing? "

"I'm alive." It's the best answer that I can give her right now.

She gives me a tight smile, and before I can say anything else, the door to the clubhouse opens, and I see a big man and a girl with him.

At first, I take a slight step back just in case this isn't someone that they know, but Boss is quick to let me know that the people that just walked in are her family. Cowboy is her man, and the girl is her daughter.

"Wow, that's amazing," I reply, doing my best to keep the envy out of my tone as I speak to the little girl.

It's nothing like I thought. For some reason, part of me believed that when I got out of that hell, I'd be able to go back to my regular life. That's not the case. Everything has changed. They've all moved on with their lives while I was stuck in a gold-plated cage, losing eleven years of my life.

The bunch of them start to talk and laugh. Acting just like a normal family, at least what I knew to be somewhat of a normal family before. Yet just the noise they're making is enough to have my hair standing on end. Everything feels so incredibly overwhelming. I can't handle it as much as I want to be out of that room and free. The thought of being out within a community like this seems to make me feel just as bad.

I turn as slowly as I can, trying to move without drawing too much attention. I slowly make my way back up the stairs and into the room. I'm so upset that I managed to get to this point in my life with pretty much nothing to show for it.

What irritates me even more, is how little of an impact my absence had, even on Dante, or Hoodrat as everyone calls him.

Everything is different. Everyone's lives have changed, and I was . . . I was just frustrated. These are the same people I thought could be my family, yet for eleven years, I had to lie there in that room every night and just wait for the next day to come. I didn't know if I was going to be alive the next day or if I was going to be sold, or even if I was going to have to stay there another fucking decade. All I know is I was waiting for cavalry that never fucking showed up because they were all here living their best lives.

"Hey Giada, is everything alright?" Dante asks as he walks into the door behind me. His voice is soft, and my initial reaction is to just turn in his arms and let him hold me, but more than that, I want some answers.

"Why didn't you come for me? Why did it take you eleven fucking years to come for me?" I turn my gaze on him, my eyes hard as I stare into his shocked face.

"What . . . I . . ." He shakes his head in an effort to try and clear his thoughts, or at least I'm assuming that. Suddenly, I felt bad that I had accused him before I found out what had actually happened. He looks like I just stuck him in the fucking eye with an ice pick with the pain on his face.

"Giada, I tried to come for you. So many times over the years. I went to look for you that day. You were supposed to meet up with me and didn't show up. I even went to your house, but your parents told me that you didn't want anything to do with me. That I was just ruining your life, and you went to college without letting me know because you were just trying to get away from me. I was a fucking mess for years, but I never stopped looking for you. I only assumed that your parents were telling me the truth, so I was looking in all the wrong fucking places," he admits, and the realization of what he's telling me dawns on me.

My parents did this to me. "My mother? My father did this to me," I ask, squeezing my eyes shut, trying to get the images of them out of my mind.

I hate this. How could they do something like this to me? How could I just allow someone to hurt me like this?

"I ran into your parents in a restaurant a few days ago. That's how I knew the DiGiovannis were the ones that had you. Your mother gave me a heads up. "

I scoff at that. "Now? More than a decade later, that's when they decided to do something."

Dante comes closer to me and wraps his arms around my waist, pulling me closer and taking my weight off my ankle. "Cut them a little slack. If they got as mixed up with the DiGiovannis, they would've died."

"They should've died then." I look up at him, making sure to let him see how serious I am. "That's what I would have done to save my child."

"I know it . . ." He leans down, dipping his head so he can get a little closer to me, but just before his lips touch mine, he shakes his head and backs off.

"You can get some sleep if you want. I'm going to

just be downstairs, then I'll come back up to sleep. I'll be right there on the couch in case you need anything," he tells me, and I just manage to give him a smile. He lets out a breath and turns on his heels to walk back down to spend some time with the rest of the people in his club.

This must be a blast from the past for him, and on top of that, he has to worry about the DiGiovannis coming after him for attempting to assist me. This isn't the reunion I had imagined in my head every time I saw him coming to find me.

Pulling the long shirt that I have further down on my legs, I turn to lay back down on the bed. The emptiness of the room is familiar to me, but it makes my heart race. I'm tired of being alone. All I can think about is the fact that I've been on my own more or less for the last eleven years.

I look over to the couch and see how small it is. There's no way he's going to fit comfortably on that, but I'm not going to tell him to go away. I want him close. I don't want to be alone anymore.

CHAPTER TWELVE

HOODRAT

We've been spending a lot of time together, and even though she's still a little distant, she's getting better. The problem seems to be that I can't find a way to reach her. Everything is so superficial. I wish there was a way for me to get her to open up to me. So far, she hasn't told me anything about what happened to her that night we found her, and every time I do ask her about anything, it seems to be a point of issue. I'm not trying to push her away even further, so I have to figure out what to do.

I thought after a while she'd just tell me, but she still hasn't said a thing.

Tonight, though, I'm determined to get her to tell me something.

I walk into the room where she spends most of her time either watching TV or reading on my iPad. She brightens up when she sees me, and I love that I still have that effect on her. So far, since she's gotten back, we haven't talked about getting back together as a couple. It's been longer than a decade, and even though I want to be with her again, it's definitely something I'm not going to push. If she wants the same things as me, she can show me.

"Hey, what are you up to?" I ask her as I walk over and sit on the bed next to her.

"Nothing much, everything okay?" she asks, putting the iPad down to address me.

She's always worrying about someone coming here for her. Fortunately, it does seem like the people at that estate couldn't tell who it was that took Giada away. If I'm wrong, they're taking their sweet time trying to come to get the rest of the crew and me.

"Everything's fine. I just wanted to check in with you. You know, see how you were feeling. The ankle?" I point down to her foot, and she wiggles it around just to show me, so it seems.

"Yeah, I don't think it's broken. It's still tender when I walk, but not as bad. Besides that, everything else is okay." She pushes a strand of hair behind her ear.

"And the bruises?" My voice is softer, and I run a hand down her thigh. It's where I saw one of the latest dark purple areas when she was getting dressed.

"They'll be fine." She starts to pull her leg away, but then she stops. "I don't know how to do this, Dante. I don't want to keep pushing you away, but anytime anyone touches me, all I can feel is him. It's like he's stuck in my head."

"You've got to get him out. Tell me what happened. Maybe that'll help." I move back a bit and give her some space.

"I don't know where to start . . . the majority of my time there wasn't so bad."

"So, tell me what happened the night we found you. You were really beat up, and if you were willing to jump out of a window to get away, then it must've really been bad." I figure this is a great place to start only because it seems like the most traumatic and the freshest out of everything that's happened.

She lets her head drop down to her shoulders for a moment before she looks back at me, "It was the first time I tried to accept my circumstances. Luigi had been coming to see me for a few weeks already, and he said that he wanted me to have some semblance of a normal life. He was treating me well. Taking me out for walks where I could never do that before. He brought me food from outside. Wooing me in my prison if you'd believe it," she says, and I do. My hands tighten up into fists, but I don't let the emotion trail up to my face.

This bastard was not only keeping her there against her will but then tried to mold her into his girlfriend. What kind of sick shit is this? I wait for my chance to speak while she continues the story.

"That last night I was there, he'd brought over some Italian food and some wine. I was having a good time with him mostly because of the wine, I think. But, still, I was laughing, which isn't something I was doing a lot of before that. So, when he started to kiss me, I let him. I was tired of being alone. He was giving me some sort of relief from my circumstances, even if it wasn't the relief that I wanted."

"I let him lay me down, and we continue to pet and touch each other. But I couldn't get into it, so I had to use my imagination." Her eyes cut to mine, and I make sure to stay focused on her. What the hell does that mean? When I don't say anything, she keeps talking.

"I imagined he was you. I mean, it was the only way I could . . . so when I did . . . you know . . . get to that point . . . I called for you. He didn't like that very much. He beat me up because I yearned for you. He said that you were scum. I thought he was going to turn out to be someone that would at least treat me decently, but it turns out he was nothing more than the rest."

I can't keep still any longer. She was beaten because she wished she was with me. I jump up off the bed and pace in front of her.

"That piece of shit is going to pay for what he did to you. I don't care how long it takes me to do it. He's going to regret ever laying a fucking hand on you," I spit out, and Giada just gives me a tight smile.

"I know you will, Dante." She stands up and puts her hand on my arm to get me to stop pacing. "You know, no matter how long I was there, I never gave up hope that you were at least still somehow looking for me. I thought the same of my parents too, so I'm happy I was at least half right."

I feel my body relax slightly, "Of course, I was still looking for you. I was angry that you'd just left me, but I still wanted to know that you were okay."

She stares into my eyes for a long while before she starts talking to me again, "Will you lay with me?"

"Now?"

She pulls me back toward the bed, "Yeah, now."

"Sure, if you want that." My palms start to sweat, and my chest tightens. This will be the closest she's let me get to her since she's gotten here.

She pushes me down in the bed, and I move over so she can lay next to me. When I watch her reach under the long t-shirt and pull her panties off, I sit up straight in bed.

"Hey, what are you doing?"

"Dante, I need you to erase him. I should have never but . . ."

"Don't do that to yourself. Anyone in your position would've done the same thing. Probably wouldn't have taken them ten years to do it either." I immediately make sure she doesn't beat herself down. She doesn't deserve it.

"Still, just having him be the last man to touch me. I don't want that to be the last memory of sex I have. Please, Dante, I need you to erase him. I need you to touch me and remind me what it feels like to have someone care for me." She crawls up on the bed and swings her legs over me. Her pussy is pressing against my cock through my basketball shorts. So warm and inviting.

All I want is to tug them down and dive right into her, but I don't want to do more damage than has already been done. "I don't think you're ready. I don't want to hurt you." I mumble, barely loud enough for her to hear me. My hands are gripping her hips like my life depends on it. I know if she starts to move on top of me, I'm not going to have any willpower left.

She whines as she drops down and peppers my face with feather-soft kisses, "I'm ready, Dante. You won't hurt me. I know you."

"Shit." The last of my self-composure snaps, and I reach up to cup the back of her head to pull her closer to me. I seize her lips, flicking my tongue against the seam to get her to open up to me. When she moans into my mouth, I attack her with a crazed frenzy. It's been so long since I've been with her. At one point in my life, I thought that I was finished waiting around for a woman that didn't want me, but it's not true.

This is the woman I want as my ol' lady. I wanted it before, and I still want it.

I lift her slightly and shove my pants off. I'm already rock hard and ready for her. Even though all I want right now is to just pick her up and slam her down on my shaft, I know that I can't. I need to make sure she really enjoys herself here. If I'm going to erase what that bastard did to her, then I'm going to have to take my time.

I pull her face back down so I can kiss her again before I flip her over, so her back is on the bed. Once I've gotten her in a comfortable position, I reach down for her shirt. At first, she's tense, but after I kiss her for a few seconds, I'm able to get her to relax.

Peeling the shirt off her body explains what she was so hesitant about. Even though most of her wounds and bruises have healed up, the ones on her midsection are still pretty bad. Mostly on two spots near her ribs. I bend my head and kiss her tenderly there. I'm going to trust her word when she tells me that she's okay.

I let my tongue run from the middle of her chest down to her cleft, where I smell her arousal. She groans out my name the second the tip of my tongue runs along her slit.

"Oh god, Dante."

I reward her, sucking and lapping at her clit until

she's writhing on the bed in pure pleasure when she lets out a high-pitched wail, and her body shakes. I know I have her exactly where I want her. I need to remind her exactly who's the one to give her pleasure. I nip and bite my way back up her body. Not hard enough to give her any pain, but enough to remind her where she is.

I slide the head of my cock against her still spasming opening, and she bucks up hard, causing the very crown of my head to slip inside of her.

"Oh fuck, G," I rasp.

She mewls, and I push into her slowly, "Who's pussy is this, Giada?"

Her eyes flutter open, and she stares at me for a moment, so I lean down and suck on the very edge of her earlobe and ask again. "Who's fucking pussy is this, baby?"

"Yours, Dante. Yes, it's yours." She wraps her legs around my waist, and I begin to pump a little faster.

"You feel how tight you are around me? How wet you get with me inside of you?" I pull back and graze my lips with hers.

"So wet," she moans out.

"You feel good, baby? Am I making you feel good?"

"Perfect. Give me more, Dante. Please," she begs

me, and I thrust harder into her. It's my job to give her exactly what she wants in her time of need.

"It's yours, Giada. Anytime you want it."

I thrust into her a little harder, and the sensation is so intense that I can't help but move faster. I don't want to hurt her, but I can't control myself.

I pump into her hard, and she grips onto me, going right along for the ride.

The both of us race toward another release. I feel the familiar buzz and spark of pleasure rushing across my skin.

Her walls ripple and squeeze me, pushing me even further toward the edge.

"I'm close, Dante. Please," she whispers, and I command myself to hold back.

I lift up, so the head of my cock rubs against her G-spot every time I pull out.

She squeals before she sucks in a deep breath and scratches her nails down my arms. Her eyes slam to mine before she squeezes them shut, and I feel her coming on my dick.

"Oh fuck. It's so good. So fucking good." I feel my balls pull up hard, and only seconds after her, I release deep inside of her.

I have to take several deep breaths before the bright lights stop flashing behind my eyelids.

If I thought I was ever over this woman, I was out of my mind. She's even more under my skin now than she ever was before.

CHAPTER THIRTEEN

GIADA

"You need another?" Faith asks as she gestures to my cup, that's already half empty. If this were last week, I'd be deep into my third cup already, but I'm finding I need less and less help to get through the tough times now. Now that I have Dante, that is. I'm still getting used to everyone here calling him Hoodrat, but I remember it started way back when. Even then, I didn't understand the meaning behind the name, but he must love it for some reason.

The music is loud, and there are quite a few people in the bar right now, but I'm surprised to see just how easy it is for me to relax. If I'm honest with myself, I'm proud of it.

Ever since Dante and I have been getting our relationship back on track, it's almost like I'm more at ease with everything. Like I'm feeling safer than I have in a long time, simply because I know he's here.

I take another sip of the drink I got for myself at the bar, and I see Dante and Ricochet walking over to me. I remember Ricochet from before I was kidnapped. He was a good guy even then. I'm not surprised to see him still here with everyone else. They're flanked by a woman with purple hair that I don't know. I don't really like to be around strangers, but I'm sure if Dante is bringing her over here, she must be okay.

"Hey G, you alright?" Dante asks, leaning over and kissing me on the mouth in front of everyone. I've never had to question whether he wanted to be with me. He always shows me just how much I mean to him.

"Yeah, I'm okay. Looks like you guys are going to have a packed house tonight," I say to Hoodrat, but my eyes dart to the side where the new woman is. I wonder if anyone is going to introduce us.

"They're savages." She rolls her eyes and sticks her hand out. "I'm Venom."

I laugh and return the gesture. "I'm Giada." She

looks tough, but when I look into her eyes, they seem warm and inviting. She's family, just like the rest of the club members in here.

"Sorry, I forget to do that shit sometimes," Ricochet says, running his hand through his hair and shooting his woman a remorseful glance. Then both he and Dante exchange a strange glance.

"You two going to be straight for a few minutes? We need to chat with Boss." I nod my head, and so does Venom. I watch as Ricochet and Hoodrat both walk off toward the back, leaving me here with Venom. If I didn't know any better, I'd think that both of them are setting me up.

"I'm guessing they shoved us together so we can get to know each other," Venom says before she reaches over and grabs a beer from behind the bar.

"I guess." I shrug and fold my hands in front of my body. It's hard to stay at ease when I have to share my space with someone I don't know. Sure, she may be family, and I may be safe with her, but I don't want to have to think about what I should say while I'm in front of her, so I don't offend or freak her out.

There's a large crash behind me, and before I can control my reaction, I spin around to see what it is.

My eyes scan the crowd, and I focus on a small punch bowl that looks to have been nudged off one of the side tables. Even though I know what it is that made the sound, my heart is already racing double time, and I feel the beginning of a cold sweat forming over my brow. I close my eyes for a few seconds, trying to stop myself from having a panic attack.

"Yup, that's why," Venom says with slight laughter in her tone.

"What the hell is that supposed to mean. That's why, what?"

"That's why they wanted us to get together. You're wearing that trauma right on your sleeve. It's fresh. Something happened to you before you got here?" Venom's brow perks up, and I glare at her for a second, trying to figure out what her angle is.

"Yeah, I was held hostage for a while. Hoodrat and a few others found me not too long ago," I have to remind myself to call him Hoodrat in front of the others in the club. They wouldn't be used to me calling him Dante.

"Shit, for how long?" Venom asks, not seeming too shocked by the revelation I just dropped for her. Anytime I hear myself say it out loud, it makes me cringe a little. I've spent more of my adult life locked up than I have been outside. I usually don't like to tell people the exact number of years because it makes them act like I'm a bit of a pity case at first. I understand their reasoning for having those feelings, though. I'd pity me too.

"Eleven years."

"Yeah, that's a fucking long time," she says, but there's no further surprise. What the hell happened to this woman that being held hostage for eleven years isn't enough to shock her? I'm not sure, but I'm curious.

"I was in a cult for a long while. They didn't let us go. I guess it's a little different because I had others around me, but I know a bit of what you're going through." We sit there for a long time, ignoring the party that starts to get more insane behind us. She tells me some of her stories about her time with the cultists. I know I had it bad where I was, but it's nothing in comparison to what she had to go through at the hands of those fucking sickos. I'm so glad that she managed to find her space here at the club. At least here, I know the club will take care of her.

"A cult?" I ask. I would've never thought that she'd be part of a cult or held hostage. She seems so put together, so calm and normal. "I would've never guessed that," I say out loud.

"Really? Well, that's good. I know when I first came out, you probably could've been able to tell just by looking at me for too long. I was always worried about someone coming back to find me or someone coming for revenge. Definitely wasn't always like this, but I found strength in my anger. Strength in needing to get my daughter back and make those bastards pay for everything they did." She laughs and takes another sip of her drink.

"Still, what you've managed to accomplish is remarkable." I push my drink back and forth on the bar between my fingers. "How did you do it?"

Venom turns her gaze on me, "How did I do what?"

"How did you heal?"

This time she downs the rest of her beer before she starts talking. "I'll be honest with you. It took me a long time, but you have to start with the first steps. If you want my advice, you have to start by taking back your power. Confront those who hurt you. Once that's done, move on with your life and be happy. It's harder than just snapping your fingers and making it all go away, but once you start on the journey, the healing gets easier."

I raise my glass to her, and we clink drinks. What she's saying is exactly what I want. I want the healing process to begin. I want someone to be able to reach out and touch me without me having a panic attack. I just want my life back.

CHAPTER FOURTEEN

HOODRAT

I'm amazed it's only been a little over a week since Giada has been back in my life. She's gotten so much better in the last week. So much so that I wouldn't have ever thought she spent the last decade locked up in some mansion prison. Every night that I lay with her, I feel the same way I did before she was taken.

I remember her always having on a special necklace before, but she said that they took it from her before she was there for a month. She didn't tell me she wanted me to replace it, but she deserves to have a replacement. She deserves to have everything her heart desires.

I intend to give it to her.

She's at the clubhouse right now, just relaxing. I told her I was going out and she should stay with the girls while I ran a few errands.

I didn't want to tell her what I'd been up to today. I want to surprise her but staying out for that long is a bit of a nerve-wracking experience. Since she's been here with me, I haven't had to leave her for more than a couple of minutes. I don't want her to need me and me not to end up being there for her.

As I was leaving this morning, Ricochet was quick to let me know I can't coddle Giada, or she's never going to get over this. I don't want her to be coddled, but I don't want her hurt either.

The ride to the jewelry shop is about twenty minutes from the clubhouse, and I'm upset to see that the fucking place is still closed by the time I get there. I have at least another thirty minutes before it opens. If I go back now and have to leave again, that might be worse, so I decide to stay and just grab something to eat while I wait.

My eyes are always scanning the area, and today's no different. While I grab an egg sandwich from the corner store, I scan all the cars and trucks around to make sure no one's following me.

I'm happy that Luigi seems to have given up on

chasing Giada, but something about it just doesn't sit right with me.

If I had used all that effort to keep someone locked up for so long, why the fuck wouldn't I be out searching for her? Not only would I want to make sure I got my property back, but I'd be worried about her going to the cops or something like that. It's not like Luigi DiGiovanni is that hard to find. If Giada decided to go to the cops with her information, it could be fucked up for him and his family. Then again, I'd be more shocked if Luigi didn't have the police in his pocket.

I'll have to talk to Boss when I get back about trying to figure out if there's any new chatter about what's going on. Everything that's happened so far seems off, almost incomplete like I'm waiting for some sort of ball to drop.

I need to make sure I do everything I possibly can to keep Giada out of harm's way. I've already lost her once. I don't know what I'd do if I ever lost her again.

After stuffing my face with the greasy egg sandwich, I take my time making it back to the jewelers. Everyone is going about their day. Families and couples enjoying the early morning.

Every few seconds, I hear a woman laugh, and

my mind instantly goes right back to the times when G used to laugh like that with me. I hate that we've missed so much time with this bullshit. Years of our lives are just gone because some asshole decided to take what was mine. He didn't just take what was mine, though, and I have to remind myself of that. He took the two of us away from each other. Luigi fucked us both.

I can only imagine where I would've been if this shit didn't happen. We might've had a kid already. Maybe a wedding if that's what she wanted. We could've bought a house. We could've had our first fucking family vacation. So much of our lives were missed out on and I have to try to make up for it now.

I don't mind making up for it or even spending all the time I can with her. What I hate is the fact that she wasn't given a choice. What if she truly did want to go to college? What if she did want to date other people besides me? What if she wanted to or did want to be a mother already? I can only give her a second-rate substitution. Luigi and his fucking asshole minions took away her choices, her time, her options. They took away so much.

When I make it to the jewelers, I see they're just opening. The woman behind the counter stared at me through the window, and I could see on her face that she was scared. I'm a big gruff looking man with a leather vest on, and I'm pretty sure my hair looks a mess. I don't really care what I look like. I have money to spend and a lot of it at that.

After a few seconds, she hits the buzzer under her display, and the door buzzes open.

"I'm sorry, sir, we don't have everything out yet. We've only just opened." She smiles, but her lips tremble slightly.

"That's just fine. I can wait a little while," I tell her and go to stand at the side.

"Um . . . well, is there something you were looking for in particular?" I can go get that from the back."

"Yeah, a necklace."

"Do you know what kind?"

"No, I was hoping you'd be able to help me out with that. I'm replacing one for my girlfriend." I say the word girlfriend, but Giada is so much more than that.

"Okay, well, give me a few seconds," the woman behind the counter says.

She rushes off to the back, and as I suspected, someone else comes out in her place. This one is a middle-aged man, a little soft around the center but bigger and more severe than the scared woman.

"My associate says you're looking for a necklace?" he asks right away, straight to business.

"Yes, I thought she was going to help me." I can't help but poke a little fun.

"She will, but we're just trying to garner what you're looking for. Gold, silver, white gold? Something thick, dainty? Diamonds? Gemstone?" he asks a bunch of questions, but before he's finished, it felt like my head was already spinning.

"Sir, if I knew all that, I wouldn't be here this early in the morning. I just want to see some of your stuff. I promise you, I'm not here to waste your time." I do my best to stay respectful. I know what I look like, and I know what the stereotypes are about people in clubs.

The longer I'm here fighting with them, the longer it will be before I can get back to Giada.

"Right, okay, well, I'll have her bring it all out, and we can go from there." He gives me a smile before he puts his hand out to shake. I'm Mr. Tummer."

"Nice to meet you. I'm Dante." I don't think giving him my road name would further my cause very much.

Within a few minutes, both of them have about two dozen trays of necklaces for me to look at. The woman behind the counter can see how confused I am, and she takes some pity on me.

"Okay, you said you wanted to replace her old necklace? Was it broken, or was it stolen? Did you want to get her something that reminds her of it or something better?"

"I think I want to get her something a little better. It was stolen. I don't want to bring up any bad memories," I admit, and the woman nods.

"What kind of jewelry do you think she'll like, something with a lot of intricate detail, or do you think she'd appreciate something a little plainer?"

"I think that she'd appreciate the plain stuff, but I don't want it to be too ordinary, you know?" I say, squinting at the lady, and she moves me down the line. Once again, taking what I'm telling her into consideration. "Oh, don't worry about that. I'm sure you'll find a wow piece in here that would still be a statement." We get down to a few single stone necklaces, and my eyes zero in on one in particular. Every time I try to look away, my eyes drift right back over to where that one is.

"This one." I poke my finger right under it, and the woman smiles brightly.

"I was hoping you'd picked that one. It's a wonderful classic piece. A garnet teardrop stone, the chain itself is double stitched, so it should be sturdy enough for continuous wear." She picks it up from the velvet tray and puts it up for me to see in the light. The way the sunlight bounces off it and the colors it splashes against the countertop makes me smile. I never expected it to be so hard for me to find something, but now that I have, I'm glad I took my time making my choice.

"Yeah, that's the one," I mutter more to myself than the woman making the sale.

"That's a great choice, Dante," Mr. Tuller says as he continues to put out the merchandise in the other displays.

"Yeah, thanks for the help." I look back over to the woman who's been helping me, "Let's get this wrapped up."

She gives me a big smile and is only a little hesitant when she lets me know that this necklace is twenty-two hundred dollars. When I put my credit card on the table without hesitation, she smiles and rings me up.

It's only a few more minutes before both of them are smiling, and I'm walking out of the store with my new necklace for my girl.

***

The minute I get back to the clubhouse, I know something's wrong. Not only is my door open to the main room, but I don't see any of the women.

The cold fear grips my throat as I rush up to my room just in case Giada is in there. I don't want to overreact for nothing.

"G?" I call out for her, but I don't hear anything.

What the fuck!

I make my way back downstairs and look for anyone else.

I rush to the side rooms and bang on the door to see if Muffler or Ricochet are here. Ricochet's the first one to come out into my sight.

"What, bro?" he asks, the sleep still heavy on his voice.

"Where the hell are the girls at?" I ask him.

"What? They're downstairs." Ricochet steps out of his room. Standing straight up now, his eyes dart around before he pushes by me and rushes downstairs.

"Fuck. I have no idea where the hell they are. She told me she was going to hang out with Giada. She didn't tell me they were all going to go out. I don't fuckin' know," he says before he storms back up the stairs.

He comes up with his phone and is doing the same as me, calling our women over and over, but none of them answer. It's not fucking possible. Did someone really just walk in here like they fucking own the place and take our ol' ladies out of here? I refuse to fucking believe that shit.

"We need to move," I bark out at Ricochet.

"Hold up, man, we don't know what's happening. They could've just gone to the store. No one of threat has been in here. This shit doesn't make any sense," Ricochet calls out as I make my way toward the door.

"No threat! If there was no fuckin' threat, then where the hell are they?" I snarl as I spin back in his direction.

"What the fuck is going on?" Boss comes out from the back.

"We don't know where the girls are. I was fuckin' asleep on the couch in the game room. We came down here, and they've fuckin' vanished."

"Uh, they didn't vanish. They walked out," Reno says from where he is by the door.

"The whole group of them walked out and said they'd be back in a bit."

"Where the hell did they go?" I storm over to him.

"I don't know. I didn't ask them. They seemed happy to go, smilin' and stuff. Out to eat? I don't know, Hoodrat," Reno answers, a bit of panic on his face. But the way he shrugs tells me he doesn't really give a shit.

I slam my eyes shut and ball my hands into fists. There's no way Giada would've gone off on her own, and if she did, we've got a lot of shit to talk about. I've been treating her with kid gloves simply because I didn't want to scare her or push her away. But if she's reckless enough to go out without any type of backup, then she really doesn't understand just how much danger she's really in.

CHAPTER FIFTEEN

GIADA

When I went to bed last night, I didn't realize just how much of what Venom said to me would be weighing on my mind. While I waited for Dante to get back from his errands, all I could think about was how right she was. It's time for me to confront those who did this to me. The same ones that were supposed to help me when I needed it. The ones that were supposed to come look for me when I wound up kidnapped. My parents.

Venom, Gold, and Abyss are sitting around drinking coffee as I finally make up my mind. I need to get my power back, but more importantly, I need answers.

I stroll up to the three of them, not really sure

how I'll be able to ask them straight out if they want to come help me get some answers, but luckily for me, Venom already knows a lot. She knows I want something before I even have a chance to say anything.

"You might as well go on and tell me what it is," she says to me, not even looking over her cup of coffee.

"What? What do you mean?" I ask, trying to keep my voice even. I hate that she knows I need something from her.

"Giada, you've been walking back and forth, probably trying to figure out a way to ask us whatever it is you want to ask us. We're all family here, so just ask. The worst that's going to happen is we're going to say no. If that's the case, then either you go do whatever it is on your own, or you wait. And if you wait, we figure out how to do it together." I lean against the table where they are sitting, and I think about the reasons for any one of them to tell me no. What would that mean for me? Either way, I'm going to do it today. So, I'm just hoping that I have some support. "I need to go to my parents' house and find out why they didn't try to look for me."

"Parents' house?" Gold asks.

"Yeah, they knew where I was, but . . . at least

that's what I got from Hoodrat, so either they didn't want to be bothered to come get me, or they just didn't want to go against Luigi. Either way, I need to find out why they made the choices that they did." I'm as honest as I can be, and Venom takes a big slurp of her coffee.

"Do you see them getting violent or anything like that?" Venom asks.

"Violent? No, not at all. My father likes to talk a big game, but the man is probably scared of a house cat." I shake my head.

"All right, let's roll." Venom pushes her cup to the side while Gold and Abyss follow along.

"You want me to come?" Gold asks.

"I second that question," Abyss adds.

"Yeah, I'd appreciate all the support that I can get. I don't want to lose my nerve. I want my answers, and the only way I'm going to get them is if I go ask them for it," I tell the group of ladies.

"Cool, you're already learning how things work in the club. It's really strong of you," Venom says with a smile on her face. I like that she thinks I'm strong. If I could become at least one-quarter of how strong Venom is, I'd be well on my way to being healed from what happened to me at that place.

I want to forget everything that happened to me

there, and I aim to be whole again. I'd like to start my life over with Hoodrat and the rest of the people in this club. I want to be able to walk out in the street and not have to worry about who's watching me or who's waiting for me. I wonder if it'll ever change if I'll ever not be looking over my shoulder and wondering if someone is going to take me back to that place. I just want to live my life and be happy.

The first step for me to do that is to find out what it is my parents knew about Luigi and the rest of the people at that mansion that took me. If they gave me to them, I don't think I'd ever be able to forgive them,

Parents don't do that to their kids, no matter what the options are.

***

The drive over to my parent's house is longer than I remember, but when I get out front, I'm not surprised to see that it's not much different. The same light blue siding. The same flowers in the planters, the same crack right under the numbers on the door. It's as if my being away didn't affect anything.

Venom, Abyss, and Gold come up to the door with me, but the closer I get to the house, the more nervous I get. This feels like a bad idea. I thought I'd be so fired up when I came face-to-face with them, but instead, I just wanted to hide and wish this wasn't my reality. What would I do if they had something to do with this? Would I ever be able to forgive them?

"Go on. We're right here behind you. You don't have to worry about anything," Venom says from behind me.

I did tell her my parents weren't violent, but she made sure to carry a blade with her just in case.

I press the small worn-down black button that activates the doorbell to my house, and after a few seconds, my mother comes to the door. She opens it with a smile on her face, but when she sees it's me, instead of her pulling me into her arms, she grasps her chest and stumbles back onto the stairs that lead up to the second floor.

"Oh . . . God . . . Giada," she whimpers before she places her hands on her face and begins to cry. I want to go to her and hold her, but to even take one step into this house hurts my soul. She knew I was missing, and she didn't do everything that she should have to get me back. In fact, she waited until last week to find someone who was going to be able to help me. If she had told Dante years ago where I was, he would've found me then. If she had told the police or anyone, maybe I would have been home a long time ago.

So, now that she's sitting right in front of me with tears strolling down her face, I can't feel bad for her. She brought that guilt on herself.

"What the hell is going on? Who's at the . . ." my father's booming voice sounds, and after a second, he pulls the door open to see me standing here.

"Giada, what are you doing here?" he asks, and his eyebrows furrow in.

"Nice to see you, dad. Yeah, I missed you too," I say and squint my eyes at him.

"Oh, Giada, don't be so naive. Does Luigi know that you're here? You know you can't be here," my father hisses out at me, and I feel the frog in my throat get bigger. Instead of him being happy to see his daughter, he's worried about fucking Luigi.

"No, he doesn't know I'm here. I came here to ask you both some questions. Though, after what I'm hearing now, I'm pretty sure I know most of the answers."

"What questions?" he barks out at me. "We don't need to answer any questions. You need to get back to where you belong, Giada. You're going to make everything worse."

"Bullshit! If you think I'll turn around and go back to that place, you're out of your mind."

"Giada, you don't understand. We didn't just let Luigi keep you for the fun of it. It was to protect you. To protect Dante."

"What the hell?" I hear Venom say behind me.

"What are you talking about, Dad? What do you mean, protect Dante?"

"Giada, our family, you included, are in a bad way. We owe a lot of money to the DiGiovanni family. One way or another, you were going to go to Luigi. Either he was going to take you and kill Dante, or take you and kill us, or he was just going to take you. If he finds out where you are, I'm sure he's going to try and make sure you don't leave ever again. His father is the one that was behind the deal in the first place," he pauses for a moment and then continues.

"I never liked Dante, never. He and his family were the lowest scum on the fucking Earth, but I knew he treated you right. I didn't want him to be killed just because of our debts. If you don't go back, Luigi's going to find out where you are and kill everyone who tries to stop him from getting you back. If we could've found a way to get you home a long time ago, we would've. You need to go back to him," my father tries to tell me, but I just blink in response. Is he really trying to tell me what I think he's telling me because if that's the case, I don't truly know what to do about the situation? I can't let something happen to Dante because of me, and I know Dante's not just going to let me walk back over to Luigi.

"What the hell kind of deal did you make?" Venom asks from behind me.

"Who the hell are you?" my father spits out, and Venom steps in front of me.

"I'm probably the only one here besides Gold and Abyss who sees that you dummies are trying to put whatever fucked up debts you have on your daughter's head. You did something to get yourselves in a jam, and now you're both over here living your best lives while she's been stuck in some prison."

For the first time since she opened the door, my mother stands up and comes storming in my direction, "You don't know shit about the sacrifices that we've made. You don't know what we had to give up." She turns her eyes to me, "I didn't know they'd take you away from me forever, but I'd do it again if it meant that I could keep you away from the craziness that is the DiGiovanni family."

I don't know what the hell to believe right now.

On the one hand, my parents should've found another way to keep me safe, but if they did do all of this to make sure that I stayed alive, I wonder what kind of problems they really have going on.

"Oh, we need to go," Gold says from behind me.

"What now?"

She lifts her phone and shows both Venom, Abyss, and me that the boys have called us at least five times. They must be at the clubhouse, and we're not. I can only imagine how pissed they'll be when we get there.

I don't even tell my parents goodbye. I just turn and rush to the car. I want to get back on safe ground, and from what my parents told me, it seems like the clubhouse might just be the last safe ground around.

CHAPTER SIXTEEN

HOODRAT

We still don't hear anything from the girls, even though I see that Gold has opened up my text message. Now it's not just me pacing back and forth. Ricochet and Chuckles are both spitting mad too.

"They're here," Reno says and opens the front door.

When the three of them walk in, it takes everything in me to keep from screaming at her right here and now.

She looks tired. Her skin is paler than it usually is, but besides that, Giada looks like she's in good condition. That erases any excuses she might've given me about getting hurt somewhere. There's no other reason for her to leave at this point and not tell me what the hell is going on.

Ricochet walks past me and grabs hold of his woman, and they walk off toward the second floor. I'm assuming he wants to be alone with her when they fight. I take a page from his book and reach out to Giada. She comes to me right away, and I basically tug her all the way to my room. Once she's safely in my room, I slam the door hard enough for her to jump in fright.

"What the fuck is your problem, G? You don't understand what the hell is happening around here?" I snap at her, my voice booming through the small room.

"Dante, just wait . . ."

"No, I'm not going to wait. You should've waited before you decided to run out without telling anyone where the hell you were going. Do you realize you got people searching for you? Do you think Luigi and his cronies just forgot you existed?"

She huffs out a breath before she presses her hands to her hips, "What, am I a prisoner here too? Both places have assholes running around, and both places I can't leave. The only difference was the mansion had a little nicer decor. If I'm to be your fucking prisoner, let me know now, Dante!"

she screams at me, and I have to snap my mouth shut.

If this were anyone else, we wouldn't be clocking where she was going or coming from. It's not her fault that some crazy asshole decided to take her as a prisoner.

She turns away from me, and I let my head fall back and stretch my neck from side to side. I don't want her to feel like a prisoner. I want her to want to be here with me. I just don't want her to put herself in harm's way.

"Giada, where did you go?"

She turns back in my direction. "I just went to see my parents. I was talking to Venom last night and realized that I couldn't just sit back and ignore what's been done to me. I needed to take my power back somehow, so I figured the first thing to do was go see my parents. I didn't think it'd be this big of a deal."

Her parents. Shit.

"G, I'm not trying to keep you hostage here. Your parents were part of all this going down. I don't know what part they played in all of this, but they had to have known what happened to you. They must have . . ."

"They did. They gave me to Luigi because,

according to them, they didn't have any other choice. They were trying to protect me. They were trying to protect you."

What the fuck, and where was I?

All arguments evaporate out of my mind, and I'm stuck looking around, trying to figure out what planet I just landed on. There's no way in hell they would have done anything to protect me from anyone.

Her father can't stand me. I'm sure if I were on fire, he wouldn't spare a mouthful of spit to help put me out.

"What are you talking about? What did they say?" I ask, and she gives me the entire story about how her parents are in a bad way with the DiGiovanni family. She tells me they didn't really have a choice. How Luigi is somewhat obsessed with her. That if they didn't give Giada to them, he'd kill me.

She wraps her arms around her midsection, and as much as I want to laugh in her face, what her parents have said may be true. Right now, I don't care. All I care about is Giada's safety and making sure that she stays safe.

She sits down on the bed with a huff and drops her head to her hands.

"I'm sorry I worried everyone. I really didn't

mean to, honestly. I just wanted to find out why this happened to me. I'm sorry." Her voice barely slips out, and I feel like shit for making her feel so bad.

I know I should be supporting her and building her up, but this shit is hard when it feels like I'm just waiting for the other shoe to drop. I'm just waiting for Luigi to show his face and try his luck so I can take him down. Now hearing that her parents were supposedly trying to keep her safe this whole time has me really worrying about what the hell's so dangerous about the DiGiovanni family that made them believe the only other option was for her to be taken hostage. I can't see that being good for anyone ever.

"You think Venom, Abyss, or Gold are going to be in trouble?" She lifts her head to ask me.

"I strongly doubt it. There may be a bit of an argument, but I don't see anyone getting in trouble. We all just wanted to make sure you were okay." I sit down next to her on the bed and place my hand on her thigh, giving it a small squeeze. "I already lost you once, G. Just thinking about you going missing again makes me so insane with anxiety. I'm not trying to suffocate you. I just need to know that you're okay." I do my best to explain how I'm feeling right now to her and hope that she understands.

"I know, Dante. This is just hard for both of us. I wish there were a way for us to feel more secure without me having to stay in your sight at all times," she sighs and lays her head against my shoulder.

I remember what I was doing before I came back home and found out that she'd left without letting anyone know.

"Hold on, I have a gift for you," I say, and she lifts her head off my shoulder while I go walk over to the side table and pick up the small jewelry box. It's not exactly how I got it from the jewelers. Once I figured out the girls were missing, I was determined to find a way to keep tabs on her. Not just because I want to follow her around, but in case something happens, and I need to find her for help.

I'll be honest with her. I just hope she can see why I needed to do something like this.

Before I open the case, I tell her how I've altered the gem.

"You know that I trust you, right?"

She tilts her head and nods.

"I'm only saying that shit because I don't want you to think that I don't. After I bought this, I had Muffler put in a small tracking chip. It blends in with the backing of the gem. No one will know it's there but you. I just wanted you to feel safe in knowing that no matter what if you needed help, I'd always know where to come for you." I wait for her reaction, and she gives me a soft smile, which I take as her not being too upset.

I open the case and pull the large garnet teardrop necklace out.

Giada gasps and stands quickly to see it. Right before my eyes, just as she reaches out for the necklace, she passes out.

"What the fuck!" I drop the jewel and catch her right before she hits the ground.

"G? Oh shit! What's wrong? Giada?" I shake her a bit, and her eyes pop open as if she didn't just pass out.

"What's the matter? What happened? Why am I on the floor?"

"You passed out? Did something happen? Are you sick?" I ask, my hands roaming over her body, looking for an injury I can't see.

"No, I'm fine. I don't know what happened." She sits up and tries to shake off the event. It's not happening this time.

"We need to go to the hospital," I say, making sure to use the most commanding voice I have right now even though internally, I'm scared to death.

"What, no way. I'm fine."

"G, you're not fine. You jumped out of a fucking window. You were in captivity for more than a decade. You could have had something going on inside your body while you were there and not even known it. You're not okay." I stare into her eyes and watch as it dawns on her that I might be right.

"Okay, I hear you, Dante. I'll go," she finally concedes. I lay there with her in my arms, holding her tight while I try to force all the messed-up things that can be wrong with her out of my mind.

CHAPTER SEVENTEEN

*G*IADA

"Dante, honestly, I really think you're overreacting. I feel absolutely fine," I tell him and huff out a breath as I slam back against my seat.

"Yeah, so fine that you passed out just by getting up from the bed? You've been in captivity for the past eleven years. We've gone over this before. You need to be checked out."

"Dante, I understand that you're worried, but I promise you I'm fine. I've been through a lot worse than this," I tell him, hoping to reassure him.

"Yeah, like what?" he challenges.

"Well, for starters, I was kidnapped and held against my will for eleven years. I was ignored, terrified, and watched like a hawk daily. So, I think I would know if I needed to go to the hospital," I say, my voice trembling slightly.

"I'm sorry, it's not going to fly, G," he says, not backing down. "I need someone to take a look at you."

I can't believe it. He thinks I'm bullshitting him. I would never lie about something like this. I need to convince him I'm telling the truth. "Dante, I'm serious."

"I know, G, that's why I'm so worried." He reaches over and squeezes my leg.

I don't want to go to the hospital because I'm afraid the doctor will find something wrong with me. I'm afraid they'll find something life-threatening, and I just got my life back. I don't want to go back to being helpless. I don't want to go back to being a burden on everyone around me.

Within only a minute of being in the car with me, I break into a full-blown tantrum. Dante doesn't seem to be affected by it at all. However, it's obvious that he's determined to make sure I'm okay, no matter what was said to him. Despite the fact that Venom decided to come along with us too, just to give me some moral support, there's not much she can do either to help me find my way out of the rut I'm in.

All I can think about at the moment is what if I go to the doctor and he tells me I have cancer or some other type of life-threatening disease, and I suddenly feel sick to my stomach. My best years would've been wasted in that fucking room while I was waiting for Luigi to kill me, or something along those lines. In all honesty, I'm not sure if I would ever be able to forgive myself or my parents for allowing myself to become such a waste of a life.

I sit alone in the waiting room after we get to the doctor's office, not wanting to be near Dante at this time as he grabs hold of the forms that I need to fill out while I wait to be seen.

"G, you know he's only doing this because he cares about you, right? Even without taking into account your kidnapping, most people get doctor's appointments once a year. What he's asking you to do right now is not unreasonable," Venom says, standing in front of me.

I glare at her until she huffs out a breath and moves over to stand with Dante.

The fact that this is a reasonable request doesn't matter to me. Or how ordinary people do the same thing when they are faced with a problem. I don't want to do it at all.

During the registration process, all the information was filled out without my input, and the paperwork was given back to the front desk without me looking at it at all. To say it infuriates me is an understatement. This is bullshit. It's like I don't have a choice again.

When Dante returns to where I'm sitting, he lifts me out of the chair and sits himself down before pulling me back into his lap so that I'm safely sitting on his lap.

"The whole point of me sitting by myself was to be able to stay away from you," I tell him through clenched teeth, trying to remain as angry at him as I possibly can.

"Yeah, that shit doesn't work for me. You can be mad all you want, but I'm not going to lose out on being able to touch you just because you have an attitude. If you want to be angry, go ahead. I'll let you be angry in my arms for as long as you like." He wraps his arms around me tighter, and I groan in frustration before I let my head fall onto his shoulder and cuddle into him. In spite of his increasingly annoying ways, I love this man.

I whisper, so as to only be heard by his ears, "What if I'm not fine?"

As he pulls away from me just a bit, he furrows his eyebrows, and his shoulders slump slightly.

Suddenly, I hear my voice crack as I utter, "What if I go in there, and they find out something is wrong with me, and before I know it, I've lost all these fucking years in the damn mansion? I just got my freedom back. I just had a chance at life. I just came back to you. I can't face them telling me that it's all gone yet again," I finally confess to Dante, and my voice is thick with unshed tears.

"It doesn't matter what they say. No matter what 'it' may be, we are going to face it together. Don't give up on me before anything even begins. Most of your time was spent fighting in that mansion, but this time, you're not alone. I'll be by your side every step of the way." He reaches up and kisses my lips, and I feel some of that strength that I'm so desperately in need of.

Within a few moments, the doctor calls us in for the examination and starts the process. It's necessary for me to explain everything that happened to me over the years, from the time that I was kidnapped to spending those years in captivity. Then I tell her about jumping out of the window. I was unable to walk correctly for a short period of time after I had fallen. As part of my doctor's regular examination, she runs a number of blood tests to determine if I have any diseases or conditions that might've developed in the past, as well as checking my urine. In the midst of getting dressed again after the appointment, she comes back in with another piece of paper for me to look at. I notice she has a mix of a happy and pensive look on her face, and I'm not sure what the reason is for that. All I know is it's making me nervous.

"I just wanted to let you know that I have just received your urine results, and I want to let you know there is a reason for your sudden dizziness and passing out," she tells me, and the knot in my stomach turns even tighter.

There's something wrong with me. As my hands grip the leather table so hard that I can feel my nails digging up into the cushion as I ask, "What? What's wrong with me?" I ask.

"There's nothing wrong with you. You're expecting a baby." She smiles tentatively as Dante and Venom turn to face me, and both look at me in awe.

There is no air in my lungs. I'm not able to speak. I'm not even able to move.

In my mind, as the doctor is giving me a bunch of information and talking about the timeframe, I can only think that this could be Luigi's child. She says it's still too early for me to know exactly when the child was conceived. I know Luigi wore a condom, but I also know that condoms break all the time, and I know in my mind I'm fighting and kicking around that it might've broken.

I don't know what the hell I'm going to do if this is his kid. I just can't do it. I don't think I'll ever be able to live with that type of situation in my life.

I suddenly realize that at some point, the doctor has stopped speaking, but that I haven't said anything to her. Venom takes a step forward, so she's right in my line of sight, and I'm forced to focus on her.

"I'm sorry, Venom. What did you say?" I ask, honestly not sure what she's been saying to me. "I was just thinking . . ."

"Would you like to go to the ladies' room with me? Can we talk?" she asks.

As I nod my head, she helps me down from the table, and I turn to leave. The shock is so over-whelming that I can hardly look at Dante or the doctor while I await the end of this horrid experience.

"Giada, I know what you're thinking, but it's not his. There is no doubt in my mind that it's Hoodrat's baby," she says before the door can even close behind us in the ladies' room. I shake my head and look away from her toward the walls. I frown at her. It would be nice if I could be as sure as she is right now about what the hell is going on, but that isn't the case for me.

As I keep my face against the wall, I hear the door to the bathroom open once more. Having someone see me at my worst is the last thing I want right now. I don't want to be seen at my worst by anyone.

A muffled sound reverberates around my head, and before I can turn around and see what Venom has to say, something wraps around my face, and everything goes dark around me.

I remember so vividly the night I was taken from outside of my home. I remember the heaviness of my arms and the darkness that surrounded me that night. I had this feeling before.

Suddenly, very softly, I hear a familiar voice. Luigi's come for me, and I don't think it'll be possible for me to get away this time.

I'm so petrified that I can't move a muscle as I hear his voice move closer to me. I know there's no escaping him this time. I'm completely and utterly helpless.

CHAPTER EIGHTEEN

HOODRAT

I swore when I heard the doctor say G was pregnant, I thought the floor was going to drop out from beneath me. I could see the shock all over her face. I want to check on her, but Venom says that it should be her. I thought she was just going to take her to the bathroom, but it feels like they've been in the bathroom for the longest time.

Muffler shows up as I'm pacing back and forth in the waiting room.

"What the hell is going on with you? You look like a fuckin' caged lion."

"Nothing. I mean . . . we did get some surprising news, and I know G's feeling blindsided."

"What the hell is that even supposed to mean? I

mean, I know you said she passed out or something. Did they find something serious?" Muffler questions, his face a mask of concern.

"Yeah, she found something. Turns out Giada's pregnant."

"Oh shit!" Muffler gets happy and brings me into a hug. "That's fuckin' awesome, brother. You're gonna be an awesome father. "

I nod my head only because I have no doubts in my mind that I will be, but I also know Giada's probably having other worries. "Yeah, thanks, man. The girls went off to the bathroom to talk, but that was a while ago. I'm gonna go check on them," I say, and Muffler's right behind me as I go try to find them.

When I get to the first bathroom around the corner and don't see them there, I don't think anything of it. I just move on to the next one. But, when I get to the two others and still don't find them there, I start to panic.

"Can you fuckin' call them or somethin'?" I hiss at him as I race up and down the corridor. Giada and I just fucking talked about her disappearing, so I know that there's no way that she'd do this shit again.

"Yeah, man, it's going straight to fuckin' voicemail. Venom too," he says.

"Shit, I'm going outside." I leave Muffler behind and run out to the parking lot of the small hospital. The car's still here, so I know she didn't try to leave that way. I run to the opposite end of the building, and while I'm huffing and puffing, I have to stop and catch my breath. While I'm catching my breath, I spot a woman sitting on the edge of a loading dock.

I squint and try to figure out who it is. It looks like Venom, but she's not moving.

"Venom!" I yell out and race in that direction.

"Hoodrat! Where you at?" Muffler calls from the front of the hospital.

"The back! Move your ass!" I scream, but I don't start running right away in the direction that I see Venom in. Instead, I'm looking around like a mad man. I don't see Giada. Where the hell is she?

When I get to the loading dock, I can see that Venom's still breathing, but she's unconscious and bleeding. On the ground next to her are both hers and Giada's phones.

"Shit! What the fuck!" I hear Muffler say behind me, and I hand her over to him.

"Venom, wake up. I need you to wake up." I don't want to shake her, but I need to know where Giada is and who did this. I have my guesses. It's got to be

Luigi. Still, I wouldn't know where to go look for him.

"Shit, who did this?" Muffler asks from behind me.

"I don't fuckin' know, but I know Giada isn't fucking here. There's only one fucking person that's looking for her right now." I reach down and pick up Venom, who's groaning, but still hasn't woken up. I carry her back into the main entrance of the clinic while Muffler gets on the phone to call Ricochet.

It's only a few minutes until my brother's there to check on his woman. He's got all the questions in the world right now for me, but honestly, I don't have any answers, and all I really want to do is find out where Giada is.

"You think Luigi's responsible for this?" Ricochet grinds out as he looks in on Venom.

"There's no other option," I say before I look over to Muffler. "The necklace? Can you track it?"

"Yeah, but we gotta get to the clubhouse. That's the only system the device is linked to," Muffler tells us.

"Get over there. I'm staying here with Venom. I know Boss wants an update, but I can't fuckin' focus right now to tell her anything more than what I've said," Ricochet says.

"Got you. Stay here and watch over her. Thanks for looking out, man." I clap him on his back once before I make my way over to the car. I need to find my woman. I promised her that while she was with me, no one else was going to harm her, and the motherfucker stole her right from under my damn nose.

* * *

THE SECOND we get to the clubhouse, I let Muffler get to work trying to track down the necklace while I have a meeting with Boss.

"You didn't see anyone creeping around the office while you were waiting for her?"

"No, but if I'm honest, I wasn't fuckin' looking. All I was fuckin' worried about was her being okay. She just had a huge shock, and I thought she needed some space. I shouldn't have let her go off on her own. Fuck man, I should've walked with them to the bathroom." I slam my hand down on the desk, pissed I let this shit happen.

"Were you going to help her squat, and piss for her too, Hoodrat? She needed a second, and that's what you gave her. It's not your fault this asshole found the right opportunity. There's nothing you could've done at that point besides what the fuck you did. Don't go beating yourself up over that shit. What we need to be focused on is finding her," Boss says, and I nod.

"Muffler's working on tracking the necklace I got her."

"Thank fuck you thought to do that shit." Boss shakes her head. "You think we need to head back up to the mansion?"

I shake my head at an absolute loss. I have no idea what the hell to do. If we go all the way up there and she's somewhere down here, we'd only be wasting time, and he could be hurting her. He could be fucking hurting the baby.

"Fuck! Ahh, fuck!" I drop my head into my hands and squeeze hard, trying to get the thought of Luigi doing anything to hurt Giada again out of my mind. I'll rampage through the fucking streets before I let him get away with hurting her again.

There's a sharp knock at the door, and Muffler walks in with his laptop. "I got a lock on the neck-lace, but you're not going to like where it is." He shows me a big bright red dot, but it's showing up in the middle of the upper east side. There are hundreds of apartments in that one square mile alone. We'd be searching for a needle in a fucking haystack.

"Shit! We can't just go in there and start kicking doors down. He'd be out or hurt her before we ever found her." I stare at the map, suddenly pissed off that Muffler's tracking device wasn't more accurate.

"I know you don't usually involve her with this business, but didn't your sister do some business with the DiGiovannis a few years ago? I thought they had a penthouse in one of these buildings?" Boss says, and she's right.

I pull my phone out of my pocket and press the icon for my sister. She answers after the third ring.

"Dante, I'm in the middle of something. I have to call you back."

"No," I snap out sharply. "Please, listen, I need you. It's an emergency and one I'm not fuckin' around on, Beretta."

"Hold on," she says, and while I'm holding, I hear her telling whoever she's meeting with that they have to meet another day, and then she's back on the line. "What's the matter?"

"Luigi took Giada. We know where he is, but not exactly. We need to find a way to get into his brownstone." Before I can even finish talking, Beretta lets me know that she's on her way to the clubhouse, and we should have a separate tracking device ready for her when she gets here. She's going to come with us to the brownstone, so we have a way in.

I know I don't say it very often, but I love my sister.

***

The drive to the Upper East Side isn't very long, but the waiting to see if anything happens is mind-numbing. We don't see any movement inside the windows of the brownstone they supposedly have. Meanwhile, Luigi's car isn't here. It could just be part of his crew that's in there or someone from his family. We need to make sure we can get in before we make any moves. The last thing I want right now is for anyone to give Luigi a heads up.

I watch from the car with Muffler as Beretta walks in. The door almost closes behind her when she tries to run back. Someone grabs hold of her hair, and I see her crumble down to the ground.

"Shit!" Muffler and I jump out of the car, racing toward my sister. Before we even get there, I see what looks like Luigi racing back inside. They're here. If he's here, that means my Giada is here too. I can only hope I'm not too late.

GIADA

When I open my eyes, I'm stuck in a dark room. It's long, and everything feels cold and hard, almost like I'm in a basement.

"Venom?" I whisper out for her, but I don't hear anything in return. Instead, the sound of footsteps comes in my direction. The dark bag that was over my head is snatched off, taking a bunch of strands of my hair. The burning sensation shoots across my scalp as I look up and see the very last face I want to see.

Luigi.

"You know I'm so fucking disappointed in you, Giada. When I saw you all those years ago at your father's accounting firm, I must admit, I was a bit obsessed with you. I had dreams for you that were bigger than anything you could've thought of for yourself. I was going to make you the princess that you should've been all this time, but at every turn, you just seem to be set on going against that plan. At every *fucking* turn, no doubt. I promise you I'm not going to sit here and be made to be a fool," he says before he tilts his head and squints at me. "Then part of me realized just how easy it was for me to get you back. You knew I would come for you, and you still made it so fucking simple. You know, I think the real reason you're here is that you have some kind of sick attraction to me. Which is fine because I've fucking loved watching you writhe and squirm day in and day out. I was never very far away."

I shake my head and can't help but scoff at his craziness, "You think you have anything on Dante? The only way you could ever get me to entertain you was to kidnap me. And even then, it took you years for that. I'm not sure why I'm still here. I'd rather jump out of another window before I stay with you again," I finish, crossing my arms over my chest.

Luigi just chuckles, like he finds my words amusing. "It doesn't matter why you're still here," he says. "What matters is that you are, and you're going to do as I say."

I roll my eyes. "What, you think you're going to play this little hostage game with me again? That's not going to work, Luigi. I'm not going to be your little puppet. No matter what kind of deal you have with my parents."

"We'll see about that," Luigi says, a smug look on his face. "I have plenty of ways to make you comply. And I'm sure you'll find them all quite . . . intriguing. If you think things were bad before, I can't wait for you to see what your life is going to look like now."

He looks me over one final time before he stands, pulling something out of his pocket, and gags me with it before he walks out of the dark gray and brown room. I'm scared. Luigi's more than just crazy. He's also well connected. And I know he won't hesitate to use those connections to make my life a living hell. I look down at the garnet necklace around my neck, and it's the only thing giving me hope at this moment. Dante told me that he'd always have a way to find me, and I never needed to worry about being lost again. I hope he's right.

I'm only praying this beautiful piece of jewelry does what it's supposed to do, and it allows him to track me. It's so cold in here, and the only heat comes from a small crack under the door. I'm freezing, and my body's cramped from being in the same position for who knows how long. I'm gagged with a dirty rag. I cry out, but it only comes out as a muffled moan. I slide back against the wall and will myself not to cry anymore. I've been through worse, and even through it all, I still managed to find Dante again.

When the doctor told me I was pregnant, I was sure that he wouldn't want anything to do with me, but even without talking to him about it, I know that's not true. Dante has loved me through everything, and that includes this baby, no matter who the father is.

The sound of heavy footsteps causes me to jump. They come from down the stairs, and I'm frozen in fear. I don't know if it's Dante or Luigi coming to kill me, but either way, my fear freezes every limb of my body. I mentally prepare myself for the pain and suffering that's about to come, and I can only hope that it will be quick. The footsteps get closer and closer until they're right outside of the room.

At that moment, my subconscious decides to start screaming in my head. It tells me that Dante and everyone else is dead. I force myself not to feed into the panic. I just need to keep my cool and stay alive.

I shriek in fear as the door to the small

mudroom is opened. The sound is soft against the gag, but I squeeze my eyes shut because I don't know who it is. "Giada, it's okay, babe. I'm here," Dante says as he falls to his knees and caresses my face, pulling the gag off. I reach my hands up slowly and wrap them around his neck before I collapse against his chest. I'm so overwhelmed by everything that's going on, but I'm so relieved when I see Dante's face. I can't help but collapse into his warm, safe embrace. He wraps his arms around me tightly, and tears stream down my face. I can't believe I'm finally safe.

"Shh, it's okay, babe. I've got you now," he whispers as he strokes my hair. I take a few deep breaths and try to compose myself before I speak.

"What happened? Where are we?" I ask, my voice shaking.

"We're in a small mudroom in a brownstone located on the Upper East Side. We have to leave in a hurry, though. Beretta's hurt," he explains.

I nod my understanding even though I'm still trying to process everything.

"What about Luigi? Is he gone?" I ask, afraid of the answer.

"For now, but we need to keep moving," he says.

I nod again and stand up. I may not be ready to

face the world again, but I know I have to be strong. I have to be strong for Dante.

I walk with him out of the small room and into what looks like the dining room. The room's in complete disarray after the gunfight. Broken glass, shattered plates, and overturned furniture littered the room. Bullet holes riddle the walls, and blood stains the floor. It's a complete mess.

On my way out of here, I notice Luigi's body on the ground. There's a gaping hole in his head and one in his chest. It's over. Finally, it's fucking over. A sick smirk curls up my lips when I know he's never going to be standing around the corner waiting for me. Luigi's out of my life for good. Now I can find out for certain what the hell he had over my parents that would make them give me up so easily, but for right now, all I'm focusing on is getting out of this place with my man.

"Hoodrat! Where you at?"

I hear Boss scream out, and Dante answers immediately. "We're here. We're coming out now."

We get out to the street, and I see the pool of blood right at the doorway. This must be Beretta's "Oh, God, you're sister? Is she okay?" I look up into Dante's face. He squeezes his eyes shut like just the question is enough to cause him pain.

"I don't know. When Muffler took her in, she wasn't waking up, and she was losing a lot of blood. I need to get to the hospital to check on her," he says, and I notice his chest rising up and down faster than normal.

"I'm okay. I promise you I am. I can stay with Boss and Abyss. You go see about your sister." He looks down at me to confirm if I'm sure, and I reach up to kiss him. "I'm okay, Dante. Go." I push him slightly, and I see him look over my shoulder at Boss before he runs down the stairs to his car.

"Come on, let's get you home," Boss says, and I follow them to their car as I watch Dante speed away. I can only pray that Beretta and Venom are okay. I don't think I can bare to lose any of my family to a fucking bastard like Luigi.

I SIT on the couch in Dante's room with my hands clenched into fists, my nails digging into my palms. I'm waiting for the phone to ring, for someone to give me any news about Beretta or Venom. The last I heard, they were lying unconscious in the hospital. I keep replaying the events of this afternoon over and over in my mind. Venom was just trying to help me, and Beretta was just trying to help her brother. Both of them could possibly die because they were looking out for me.

And now here I am, waiting for news that may or may not be good. I feel helpless and alone. I wish I had gone with Dante to the hospital. I wish I could be there with them now. The phone finally rings downstairs, and I race to open the door, my heart in my throat. Boss answers it but doesn't say anything to me. Her eyes come up to where I'm standing at the top of the stairs, and she gives me an understanding look.

I meet her halfway as she makes her way up the stairs to me, "Why don't you come down and eat with us? I'm sure the guys will call us when there are any changes," she tells me, and I want to be as optimistic as she is, but I can't bring my mouth to turn into a smile. I don't want to eat right now, but I don't want everyone else to feel like I'm pulling away from them.

I get down to the table, and most of the food is already spread out. Before I even have a chance to sit down, Destiny, Boss's five-year-old, starts to talk my ears off. Within seconds all the heaviness and anger I was feeling a second ago evaporated from my body. How can I keep it when I have to try and keep up with what this little girl is saying? I'm laughing before long, and there's a little voice in my mind that reminds me in a few months, I could have a daughter just like her.

All in a matter of weeks, my life has changed, and it'll continue to change. The only thing that remains the same is my love for Dante. This growing child inside my belly is just more proof that no matter what, our love can overcome anything.

CHAPTER TWENTY

HOODRAT

The hospital waiting room is a small, cramped space with faded walls and a musty smell. The chairs are old and uncomfortable, and the floor's covered in a thin layer of dust. There are several other people in the room, all of them with family members who're waiting for news about their loved ones. The atmosphere's tense and anxious, and the only sound is the occasional muffled sob.

My sister has been in a coma for three fucking days now, and the doctors say that her brain is recovering from the swelling, but they're giving her a good prognosis. But how can this be good? She was hit in the head with a stone statue, and while it might've been small, the hit she took was a hard one.

Fuck, then there's the guilt. I willingly put my sister at risk, but I didn't have a clue this was going to happen.

I sit in the waiting room day after day, waiting for some news, *any* news really. The nurses come in and out, but they never have anything new to tell me. I try to read or watch TV, but I can't focus on anything. I just sit here and wait. And worry.

What the fuck am I going to do if she dies?

I always thought there would be more time. Time to tell her how much she meant to me, time to express how grateful I was for her presence in this life. But now, as I look through the window at her sleeping form in the hospital bed, I know there may not be much time left.

She wasn't always the nicest person in the world, but we did have some happy times together. Still, when I needed her, she was always there for me, no matter what. And now, I may never have the chance to tell her how much she means to me, how much I love her. The worry consumes me as I walk out of the waiting room and go to sit by her bedside. I hold her hand tight, hoping that somehow, she can feel my love and strength through this dark time.

After a few minutes, the door to her room swings open, and I jerk my eyes in that direction. It's Abyss.

"Shit. Sorry, I didn't mean to scare you, man," Abyss says before walking closer to me. "Damn, brother, you look like shit."

"Yeah . . . well, in case you haven't noticed, my sister's in a coma. I'm not feeling like my best self right now."

Abyss sighs before she sits on the edge of the bed, careful not to bump Beretta, "I know, man. This shit's rough all the way around. I'm glad Venom woke up but having Beretta like this cuts all of us deep."

"It is," I say as I look over at Beretta. "I just feel so helpless right now. I want to do somethin', but I don't know what to do."

"I know how you feel," Abyss says. "But sometimes we just have to be patient and wait. Beretta's a strong woman, and I know she'll fight her way back to us."

I nod my head, "I know, it's just hard."

"I know," Abyss says as she stands up and puts a hand on my shoulder, "But don't give up hope. Beretta is a fighter, just like your woman Giada." She gives me a pointed look, and I know why.

It's not so much that I've been avoiding Giada, but I've only been seeing her for a few minutes at a time. I don't want her to be at the hospital with me because even though Luigi is dead, we don't know if the rest of his family will retaliate. I can't handle something happening to her, too, while I'm trying to deal with what's going on with Beretta.

"Fucking hell, I just can't let anything happen to her, Abyss. I can't protect her and protect my sister. I feel like I'm being stretched too thin. It feels like somewhere someone's going to get hurt because I wasn't there to help them."

Abyss says softly, "But you're not alone. We're all here for you."

It dawns on me that ever since I started this journey to get Giada back in my life, I've been trying to do everything on my own. That's not the case. My whole family's standing right beside me, just waiting on me to tell them how they can help me. I should have realized that when Boss, Muffler and Abyss showed up at the brownstone to help me when they figured out what I was doing.

They're always by my side. Right now, I need Abyss to help me so I can go talk to my woman.

"Hey, you think you can stay here for a little while? Just in case anything happens. I need to go to the clubhouse for a little while, and I'm not really trusting these doctors to let me know anything."

Abyss nods her head before she grabs the other

free seat in the room and plops down. "I got a whole real housewives episode or two to catch up on. Go handle your business, Hoodrat," she says and pulls out her phone.

"Thanks. I appreciate it."

"No thanks needed. We're fuckin' family." She dismisses me, and I give my sister's hand one final squeeze before I rush downstairs to my bike.

***

The clubhouse is quiet, and I head straight to my room. Giada's sitting on my bed with a book in her hand. She gets up fast when she sees me and wobbles slightly. I put my hand out to catch her.

"Sorry, are you okay? Any news?" She looked so worried, and I realized that was partially my fault. I've been so occupied with keeping her safe that I forgot to let her know everything's going to be all right.

"She's still the same. How are you, G?"

"Me, oh, I'm fine. I'm worried about you and your sister."

I smile and pull her into a tight hug. I feel the soft contours of her body against mine as we embrace, and I breathe in the familiar scent of her hair. She feels so good in my arms after being away from her for so long. I caress her back gently, and we rock back and forth together, savoring the moment. She was almost taken from me again. I could've lost her before I even had a chance to explain to her how much she means to me.

And how much this baby means to me.

I pull back slightly so I can look down into her eyes, "G, I want to talk to you about the baby."

I feel her stiffen, but I don't let her go. "I'm not stupid. I know the doctor told you they can't be sure of the time frame yet. Whatever you want to do about it, like either staying pregnant or not, it's your decision. I just want you to know no matter what happens *if* you choose to have this baby. It'll be mine. I already know I'm the father, and there's nothing anyone can say that'll ever convince me otherwise."

She clamps her hand over her mouth, and her eyes start to water, "Do you mean that? Are you sure you want this?"

"I want it, yes. I want to help you pick out small-ass baby clothes. I want to change diapers and fight about whose turn it is to wake up in the middle of the night. I want to see your belly grow big and you glow with that new life inside of you. I want to be here in every way for both you and this child." I kiss her gently as the tears start to fall down her cheeks.

"Oh, Dante. I love you so much."

"I love you too, Giada," I say right as I press my lips to hers. The kiss quickly turns from sweet to passionate.

I push her back toward my bed, taking a second to look over my shoulder to make sure the door's closed. I don't think my family's going to want to walk in on what I'm about to do to my woman.

When the backs of her knees touch the bed, I let her fall backward. She quickly takes off her clothing while I do the same, trying my hardest to keep her in my sights. If I could never stop looking at her again, I'd do just that.

I can't help but grin as I see the way Giada's looking at me. She wants me, and I can tell. I move closer to her, gently kissing her neck as my hands run up and down her body. She moans softly as I tease her. Moving lower, I take one of her breasts into my mouth. She gasps as my tongue circles her nipple, teasing it before moving down her body.

I gently push her legs apart and settle between them, my tongue finding her clit and teasing it softly. She moans and grabs at my hair, her body shuddering as she comes. I don't stop though, pushing her further as I lick and suck her. She tastes so sweet, and it only makes me want more.

I move lower, kissing my way down her stomach

until I reach her pussy. I lick teasingly at her entrance before slipping inside, my tongue thrusting deep. She tastes so good, and I want to make her come over and over. She is moaning now, her hips moving against my mouth as she comes.

I don't let her rest, though, flipping her over and pushing her up onto her hands and knees. I move between her legs, pushing myself inside her deep and fast. As soon as I slide inside of her, I can tell that she's wetter than ever before. Giada moans as I thrust deeper into her, our bodies moving together in perfect harmony. Her every movement driving me fucking wild.

"You're so fuckin' tight," I growl, my body slamming into hers with each thrust. "I could fuck you all day."

"Please," she begs, her body quivering on the brink of another orgasm, "don't stop."

I pound into her harder, my breathing ragged as I near my own climax. "I'm not going to," I promise her. "I'm never going to stop."

I can feel her tight walls gripping me as I move in and out of her, each thrust harder and faster than the last. She cries out as I finally reach her sweet spot, her body shaking with pleasure. I continue to move my hips, giving her everything she needs.

She's panting now, her body covered in a thin sheen of sweat. I can feel her tightening around me, her orgasm building. I lose myself in her as she finally comes, her body shaking and trembling with pleasure. She cries out, her body shaking as she rides out her orgasm. I pound into her, finding my own release and filling her with my seed.

I pull her down against me and just revel in the way our fast-beating hearts pound against each other.

I've missed out on more than a decade with her, and in all that time, I never once thought I could feel something like this. Giada is so much more than just someone from my past. She's every part of my future.

EPILOGUE

BERETTA

The sound of a resilient beeping keeps sneaking into my dreams. It would be great if someone could turn off whatever it is that's on. Honestly, I'm so sleepy that I don't know what to do. Getting some more rest is all I want right now.

My memories are coming to me in waves. At times, I remember the feeling as if someone was pulling my hair and me desperate to get back to my brother, but other times, I'm not sure if it was something that really happened or if I'm just recalling memories.

As soon as I wake up, I'll ask him about it.

There's something rough that squeezes my hand, and even though I'd like to squeeze back, the energy to do so just doesn't exist within me. My entire body is in pain, and I just want the pain to end as soon as possible. Although I'm not the kind of person to give up easily, this is becoming too much for me.

For the longest time, I've been acting hard and keeping everyone at a distance, but it's so taxing. It's almost impossible to be the cold-hearted bitch everyone thinks I am. Of course, I'm about my money and my business, but there are times when I don't want to be the one in control. Sometimes, all I want is to be able to relax and be completely submerged in the ocean of love at all times. It's not going to happen.

When the beeping disappears, my mind drifts back down into a calm, dream-like state, and I feel myself drift back deeper into my sleep.

"Babe? What are you doing over there?"

When I turn my head around, Muffler's stretched out on a couch that I don't recognize. I don't think it's at the clubhouse or at my house. It's somewhere else. What's going on here? My mind tries to work out what to do next, but Muffler calls out again for my attention.

Not my name, but *Babe*.

Never in my life have I wanted to hear someone call me that. But somehow, I want him to do it again.

My mind ignores the fact that I have no idea where I am, and I walk back to where he is to try and figure that out.

In the process of pulling me down with him on the couch, he kisses the side of my neck, which causes me to laugh freely, so I lean into his arms and lean into his embrace.

"What are we doing here? I don't know where we are," I ask him, and he just turns my head and kisses me, ignoring my questions.

I feel myself giving into what he wants. Me. Muffler holds me close to his body and squeezes me against his body, and this time when I press against him, I feel something between us. A round ball right at my stomach.

I'm pregnant? No. That can't be. How did I get pregnant?

"Easy, babe. You know the doctor told you we needed to keep you calm." He rubs my belly with all the love in the world in his eyes.

"Muffler? What's going on? I'm so confused," I whisper against him, letting myself feel all the vulnerability.

"You don't have to be confused. You're here with me. Together," he tells me as he kisses me once more. I know I should be more upset or try to find out more information about what's going on, but right now, just having him near me is enough to make me relax.

This is exactly what I want. I want love and happiness. I want Muffler.

I never let him know before how much I wanted to keep him in my life. I never could gather enough courage to tell him just how deeply I felt. I'm so sorry that I couldn't.

Almost as though the entire world is aware of how guilty I feel, Muffler's suddenly ripped out of my arms, and I am overwhelmed with a sense of grief and loss that rips through me. In an instant, instead of sitting comfortably on the couch in the warm living room, I'm standing in a cemetery. It's heartbreaking to see everyone from the clubhouse in mourning as we gather in front of a headstone. It's Muffler's.

I scream at the top of my lungs, trying to get to the fresh grave. I fall down on the ground and lay on the dirt. I want to see him one more time. All this time, I could've been in his life the way I know I should've been.

"Please! Please! I just need a little more time!" I cry out as I claw against the dirt and realize I'm no longer pregnant. I've lost everything just that quick.

Please. This can't be real. It can't.

I just want Muffler.

"Muffler."

"Holy shit! Beretta? We're here. We're right here!" I hear someone talking, and suddenly instead of being in the cemetery, I'm lying in a hospital bed. The room is bright, too bright for my eyes, so I squeeze them shut once again.

That awful beeping is back, and I realize that's what I heard before. All of that was a dream. It was the best and worst dream all at once.

It showed me exactly what I wanted with my life and also let me know just how easy it'll be for me to lose it.

COMING FROM THE IRON
VEX MC

Hoodrat and Giada's story might be over, but this is hardly the end of the Iron Vex MC.

As you may have figured out, Muffler and Beretta's story is next.

Make sure you pre-order their book here.

Full Throttle

Elizabeth Knox & Iris Sweetwater

The Clans

Elizabeth Knox & Elle Knox

One Standalones

Elizabeth Knox & E.C. Land

Raiders of Valhalla MC

Deathstalkers MC

Pins & Needles: Moscow

DeLancy Crime Family

Stonewall Dynasty

Elizabeth Knox & Raven Scott

Mafia Heirs: The Gallaghers

Elizabeth Knox & Emily Sharp

(Co-writer has changed to Rae B. Lake as of Summer 2022)

O'Dea Crime Family

SOCIAL MEDIA

Facebook
Facebook Reader's Group
Bookbub
Amazon
Goodreads
Instagram